About the Edit...

Stephen Jones is the winner of t... the Horror Writers of America ... eight-time recipient of The Britis... time columnist, film-reviewer, televisiʊɪ ... and horror movie publicist (both *Hellraiser* films, *Grave Misdemeanours*, *Nightbreed*), he is the co-editor of *Horror: 100 Best Books*, *The Best Horror from Fantasy Tales*, *Gaslight & Ghosts*, *Now We Are Sick* and the *Best New Horror* and *Dark Voices* series. He has also compiled *The Mammoth Book of Terror* and the non-fiction volumes *Clive Barker's The Nightbreed Chronicles*, *Clive Barker's Shadows in Eden* and *James Herbert: By Horror Haunted*.

David Sutton has been writing and editing in the fantasy genre for more than twenty years. He has won the World Fantasy Award and eight British Fantasy Awards and his short fiction has been published in such books and magazines as *Best New Horror 2*, *Final Shadows*, *Cold Fear*, *Taste of Fear*, *Skeleton Crew*, *Ghosts & Scholars*, *Grue*, *2AM*, *Kadath* and others. He is the editor of *New Writings in Horror and the Supernatural* Volumes 1 and 2 and *The Satyr's Head & Other Tales of Terror*, and co-compiler of *The Best Horror from Fantasy Tales* and the *Dark Voices* series. His first novel is *Earthchild* and he is currently working on a second, tentatively titled *Feng Shui*.

FANTASY
Tales

Edited by
STEPHEN JONES
and
DAVID SUTTON

Published by
Robinson Publishing
11 Shepherd House
Shepherd Street
London W1Y 7LD

Vol. 13
Issue No. 7
Winter 1991

Editor: Stephen Jones
Associate Editor: David A. Sutton
Managing Editor: Alexander Stitt
Publisher: Nick Robinson

Editorial Correspondence
Manuscripts should be addressed to David A. Sutton, 194 Station
Road, Kings Heath, Birmingham B14 7TE, UK. *All manuscripts are
welcome but must be accompanied by a stamped, self-addressed envelope
or they cannot be returned.*

Artwork Correspondence
Examples of artwork should be addressed to Stephen Jones, 130 Park
View, Wembley, Middlesex HA9 6JU, UK. *All examples of artwork are
welcome but must be accompanied by a stamped, self-addressed envelope
or they cannot be returned.*

Cover illustration copyright © J.K. Potter
ISBN: 1 85487 064 5
Typeset by Selectmove Ltd, London
Printed and bound in Great Britain by
Cox & Wyman Ltd., Reading, Berks.

CONTENTS

THE CAULDRON

As this volume's *FT Forum* reveals, writers in the horror/dark fantasy genre frequently use psychic research as background material for their books and stories. British author Peter James is following in a long and distinguished tradition of authors who use real-life experiences of the supernatural as a basis for their fiction.

However, the question often arises (most notably in the tabloid press or from those who believe that the genre is corrupting): is horror fiction harmful? Can reading stories about monsters and mutilation turn you into a drooling psychopath with no will-power of your own?

Most people will accept that art reflects life, not the other way around; therefore there is already plenty of ammunition to fend off the accusation that the genre corrupts those who read or watch such material.

Two notable examples, Shakespeare and Dickens, used madness, mayhem and murder (as well as the supernatural) extensively in their work, but they still drew their stories from life. Horror fiction and movies do not invent the terrors they display, they all too tragically reflect the world we live in.

But while physical violence and psychological menace are there for the writer to extrapolate from, what about the psychic? We all know that people mutilate each other, but do we also dream the future, can we remember previous lives, are some people able to control the movement of objects with their mind? If parapsychology doesn't exist, then authors using such research are not reflecting reality but embroidering a myth (much as the writer of Arthurian fantasy might add to the legend of the Once and Future King—if you believe Arthur was purely fictitious).

1

However, as with all such myths which are embedded in our collective unconscious, the psychic world is disposed to hang on with amazing tenacity.

It's easy to dismiss it out of hand: you may never have researched the subject, or you may be unable to accept what often appears to be flimsy evidence. Yet, as anyone who has read the literature will testify, the evidence is *not* always that flimsy. Many thousands of individuals—probably millions if you count those who have not told their story—have experienced the paranormal, from déjà-vu to telekinesis. Many have travelled beyond their bodies. Many have been given a glimpse of the future.

Can we afford to dismiss the weight of much of this evidence because it wasn't observed under controlled conditions? If you believe the sceptics, then everyone who has ever had a psychic experience, throughout recorded history, has been duped by his or her own mind, fooled by misinterpretation, or suffered a temporary breakdown. It seems unlikely, doesn't it?

Writers who utilise psychical research in their fiction are entering into one of the most imaginative and as yet unexplained aspects of life—along with such questions as Does God Exist? and How Was the Universe Created? (In fact, modern physics is surprisingly close to accepting certain premises of the paranormal).

Dreams, visions, ghosts, reincarnation, precognition, clair-voyance—these, and many more, are the so-called fictional "myths" that perhaps hide a reality which we stand on the brink of understanding. Writers who use psychical research are not inventing terrors of the unknown but simply dipping into the waters of life. No harm, but much insight can come from their observations.

The literature of the *fantastique* is uniquely placed to expand the limits of our perception. As our unending demand for knowledge continues, the best genre fiction will reflect our ability to question what we are told, and feed the imagination that allows us to accept that the unknown is nothing to be afraid of.

The Cauldron

*

Congratulations to Jean-Daniel Breque, Kim Newman and Steve Rasnic Tem who have each had stories from *Fantasy Tales* chosen for the 1990 "Year's Best" anthologies, *Best New Horror 2*, *The Year's Best Horror Stories XIX* and *The Year's Best Fantasy and Horror: Fourth Annual Collection*. That's an achievement that few other titles can match, and it just goes to prove that *Fantasy Tales* continues to present the very best in fantasy and horror fiction by established stars and newer names in the genre.

The Editors

Peter James

FT FORUM:
THE SUPERNATURAL —FICTION & FACT

Peter James lives in Sussex with his wife, Georgina, their Hungarian sheepdog and the ghost of a Roman centurion. After a film school training, he founded an independent film production company in Canada where he made eight films, including Deranged, Children Shouldn't Play With Dead Things *and the award-winning* Dead of Night. *On returning to England he formed a new company to make the fantasy adventure* Biggles *and edited the picture book of the film,* Biggles—The Untold Story. *More recently he has published three acclaimed novels,* Dreamer, Possession *and* Sweet Heart, *and he has just completed a fourth,* Twilight. *In each of his novels, Peter writes about a different area of the supernatural/paranormal and he has developed a reputation for his meticulous—and frequently frightening—research, which*

5

give his books a strong ring of authenticity. Here he tells the true story that triggered his curiosity in reincarnation, the subject of his most recent novel, Sweet Heart, *and gives us an insight into the background research for that book . . .*

An Australian woman had a frequently recurring dream throughout her life. The dream was always the same. She was in the garden of an English country house, walked through a brick archway, and up into the woods above, carrying something. She would stop at a point in the woods and place what she was carrying in a deep hole in the ground. Then she would wake.

In 1965 she and her husband came to England, for the first time, for a motoring holiday. Travelling through Dorset they passed a house identical to the one in her dream, and she told her husband to stop the car. Ignoring his embarrassed protestations, she insisted they drove in.

The owner came to the front door, an affable old boy whose family had owned the house for generations. When she described to him the garden with its archway, and other parts of the grounds in detail, he was astounded. The garden was indeed as she described it—once—but not now; it had been changed over fifty years ago. But the woods were still the same.

He accompanied them for a walk through the grounds and in spite of the changes, she had an immensely strong feeling of familiarity with the property, and as they walked up into the woods, she felt as if she had last been in them only a few days before, at most. She led them to the spot where she had always carried the objects to in her dream and suggested they should return with spades and see if there really was anything there.

Half an hour later they uncovered a small cache of gold and silver relics. Subsequent investigations revealed these items had been buried by monks from a local priory during the Dissolution of the Monasteries in 1536.

Many of us have at some time had that curious feeling of déjà-vu (Art: Dallas Golfin)

The story of the Australian woman fascinated me. She had no explanation for how she knew what she did; she had had no other glimpses into the past before this instance and was very frightened by it. How did she know this treasure was there? No one else living did. If there is any rational explanation (other than hoax, which I believe is unlikely in this instance) it may be either that trace memories of the burial of this treasure had somehow been passed down to this woman, perhaps in her genes—her ancestry was English—or that *she really had lived before.*

I determined to devote as much time as it took to try to satisfy myself whether it is possible for some part of the souls/spirits/personalities of people who have died to return here on earth and be born into new physical bodies; or whether there is another explanation for this story and many others, equally inexplicable I subsequently came across in my research.

"I've been here before!" Many of us have at some time had that curious feeling of déjà-vu, as we are struck by a sense of familiarity about a place we have never been to before, or a face of someone we have never met before or a conversation we are convinced has taken place before. Mostly it's gone in a flash and we forget about it. But there are children who have, at a very early age, knowlege or skills that it is almost impossible for them to have learned in their few short years of life. Children who can speak fluently languages they have never heard, who can visit a town for the first time in their lives, yet know their way around in detail and even identify some of the residents, draw landscapes they have never seen or, like Mozart, compose music at the age of 5. Often these abilities fade after about the age of 7, even in the rare cases when they are encouraged by their parents.

In 1956 Joanna and Jacqueline Pollock, aged 11 and 6 were walking down a street near their home in Hexham, Northumberland, with their mother, when a car mounted the pavement and killed them both. Their mother survived and eight months later became pregnant again, subsequently giving birth to twin girls. From a very early age, these twins displayed extraordinary personality resemblances to their dead sisters. The older twin had the personality of Joanna and the younger of Jacqueline. The younger had an identical birthmark to the dead Jacqueline's, and a second birthmark on her forehead that corresponded exactly to a large scar Jacqueline had had.

Both twins were able to describe trivial things their parents had done long before the accident. They discovered a box of their sisters' toys in the attic and pulled them out as if they had found long lost friends, each taking the corresponding toys to their dead sisters, and calling them by the same names their dead sisters had called them. One day, aged four, they were walking with their mother down the same street where their sisters had been killed and both suddenly screamed in panic about a car coming at them, and ran out of the way.

The twins are now grown up and no longer have any recall whatsoever. So how did they come to have it then? Had they picked up their mother's thoughts whilst in the womb? Inherited something in their genes? Received telepathic thoughts from their mother after they were born? Or are they a genuine case of reincarnation?

Four years ago if asked whether I believed in reincarnation I would have given an emphatic *no*. Now I would have to say there is evidence that has intrigued me, spooked me and baffled me. This particular period of research has been a strange odyssey, during which time I have been hypnotised into numerous alleged past lives, and rebirthed back into my mother's womb. I have read extensively, studied religions and philosophies and talked both to clergymen, and to many other people ranging from total sceptics to the utterly convinced, and I have tried to keep a detached view.

By far the most intriguing aspect of my research—and which I have used pivotally in the novel—was regressive hypnosis. There are thousands of documented case studies on people

9

reliving past lives under hypnosis. Among my own previous lives I appear to have been a Spitfire pilot in the Second World War, a fishmonger in Hull who died when a crane fell on me, a Frenchwoman who was murdered by a lover, a writer in 17th-century London and the primitive native of a South Seas island.

Is regression real? Or is the mind fantasising? The evidence suggests a combination of the two. Clergymen to whom I talked cannot agree about reincarnation either. The clergy has always had an uneasy relationship with the supernatural. Christianity treads an uneasy path on reincarnation. Pre–existence is an accepted tenet ("Before Abraham I was . . . The soul that was in Jesus chose the good before it knew evil," etc) but reincarnation is a no–no—except for Jesus who came back and ate with his disciples in order to prove he was not a ghost. In the way that religion needs to justify its anomalies, and ties its logic into knots in the process, Christianity seems to think it's OK for us to have lived before, and even for the dead to come back to life, provided it's in our own bodies. Could poor Frankenstein ever have been confirmed C of E?!

Postscript

There are some eerie postscripts that have happened since finishing *Sweet Heart*, and since its hardback publication: the first has to do directly with the plot of the novel, which is the story of a married couple, Tom and Charley Witney, who have decided to move out of London to the country. When they get the particulars of Elmwood Mill in Sussex, Charley has an odd sensation of déjà-vu. But when they go to view the property, although she again gets a strong sense of familiarity, she believes it must be reminding her of somewhere else, because the house that keeps coming into her mind has a distinctive stable block, which Elmwood Mill does not.

They buy the house, and shortly after moving in Charley visits a widowed neighbour, who tells her that her late husband was a keen amateur painter, and one did a fine watercolour of Elmwood Mill. She produces it, and Charley is freaked: in the grounds, exactly where she had imagined it, is a stable block. The neighbour explains that the stable block burned down in 1953.

I used a real mill house property as my model for Elmwood Mill, which I saw by chance one day and approached the owners to ask their permission to use it. They were very co-operative, but never asked me about the plot of my novel until I had almost finished, and was out there one day, checking details for the proofs. I told them that my fictitious mill house used to have a stable block that burned down in 1953 and showed them the area in the garden where I had placed it. They both became very quiet. The husband went out and returned with a set of plans of the house from the '40s. The plans showed a stable block in *exactly* the spot I had placed my fictitious one. And he told me it had burned down in 1953!

The second eerie occurrence is of an even more personal nature: in the novel, soon after the characters move in, it becomes evident that there is a presence or ghost in the house. During the writing, unintentionally but coincidentally my wife and I, who like my characters in my novel, have always been townies, moved to a house in the country. It was not until a few days after we were settled in that an elderly lady in the village cheerily informed us that the property has a ghost!

The third occurrence has only just happened. I was telephoned by a couple in Wales who told me of strange and terrifying occurrences taking place at their house—which they had recently moved into. They promised me I would not be wasting a journey in visiting them. They were right. The parallels with *Sweet Heart* were uncanny.

Almost immediately after moving in they began to feel a malign presence in the house. It worsened and life became intolerable. Unsure what to do they called in first a priest, then a medium who informed the husband that he was being haunted by the ghost of someone he had angered in a previous life . . . as is Charley, my main character, in *Sweet Heart*. Their electricity had gone haywire, producing bills of a size the electricity board could not explain . . . as happens in *Sweet Heart*. There were smells, cold eddies of air, and footsteps that mimicked those of the couple . . . just as in *Sweet Heart*!

And some people insist life does not imitate art?

Ramsey Campbell

THE PIT OF WINGS

Ramsey Campbell's 'The Sustenance of Hoak' and 'The Changer of Names', the first two stories of a sword & sorcery quartet featuring the warrior Ryre, were published in previous volumes of Fantasy Tales. *Britain's most respected horror writer, Ramsey has recently published a novella,* Needing Ghosts *(Legend/Century Hutchinson), and a full-length book,* Midnight Sun *(Macdonald), his fifteenth horror novel since 1976. His short stories have been published extensively in most of the major magazines and anthologies, including* The Mammoth Book of Terror, Dark Voices 3 *and a special* Ramsey Campbell *issue of* Weird Tales. *This year sees the publication of a new collection,* Waking Nightmares *and a comic novel about a serial killer,* The Count of Eleven. *Also worth noting is* Best New Horror 2, *which he co-edits with Stephen Jones for Robinson/Carroll & Graf. In the story that follows, Ryre rides into trouble in the slave town of Gaxanoi . . .*

Since before dawn Ryre had been riding through the forest. Except that he disliked sleeping on the move, he would have trusted himself to his steed. Instead he sought calm at the centre of himself, as he'd begun to learn to do. But the

13

oppression of the forest clung to him. Time had drowned in the green depths.

Great leaves sailed by above him. Each was shaped like an inverted ribbed umbrella spiked on a massive trunk, and each was broader than the stretch of his body from toes to fingertips. As the trunk mounted, so the leaves dwindled; the highest would be no wider than Ryre's head. But he could see none of this. Beneath the unbroken canopy of the lowest leaves, even the dawn had been no more than a greening of the dimness.

The forest road was a tunnel formed by cutting leaves; once cut, they never grew again. They rustled, withered, beneath his steed's pads. The constant sound distracted him as he listened for a hint of the sea, a breeze to stir the stagnant air.

Sometimes, especially before dawn, he'd heard a flapping high above him. It must be the gliders—the highest leaves which, having shed scales of themselves, drifted away bearing seeds. But could those leaves make such a large lethargic sound?

Now he was caged by a lingering clamour of rain. He'd heard the storm coming, high and distant at first, advancing and descending through the forest. He could only shelter close to a trunk while the deafening rain poured down the trees, turning the leaves into basins of fountains. Above him the great leaf had shivered repeatedly beneath the onslaught; he'd feared drowning. Though the storm had moved on hours ago, its sounds remained. Drips seeped through the foliage to water the roots, to tap Ryre on the shoulder, to stream down his face, to coat and choke him with humidity.

He shook his head, snarling like a trapped beast—like the beast whose emblem was the V-shaped mane which widened from his shaved crown to his shoulders. He felt helplessly frustrated by the eternity of forest, the suffocating luxuriance that seemed triumphant as a mocking conqueror, the sounds whose sources he could never glimpse. He yearned for an adversary to fight.

14

Then the vases swayed, and showed him the figures whose cowled heads he'd glimpsed reflected in the sea. (Art: Jim Pitts).

15

Suddenly he put his hands over his mount's eyes. The creature halted obediently. Ryre strained his ears; impatience gripped his brow. Yes, he had heard the sound. Amid the creaking of leaves, the soft plop of rain on the decayed forest floor, the chorus of descending splashes as high leaves drooped beneath the weight of rain, there was a distant jaggedly rhythmic thudding: axes cutting trees.

So he was nearly free of the forest. Yet the sound was not altogether heartening. As he rode forward he began to hear the dragging of chains, the cut of a whip. The oppression was lifting with the leaves, but now it was anger that shortened his breath.

Where the road dipped, he saw them. Young men whose arms looked massive as the trunks they chopped, older men whose skin was more scarred, a few brawny women, all naked except for a strip of hide protecting the genitals: there must have been a hundred of them, toiling in small groups at the edge of the forest. From their fetters, long chains trailed toward the town which Ryre glimpsed beyond the trees. Beyond the town the sea burned calmly as sunlight trailed over the horizon.

Men, dressed like the slaves but bearing whips and swords, stalked about or squatted in shade. Most looked bored, and flicked their victims as they might have lazily fingered an itch. One stood over a fallen slave. A fresh weal glistened rawly on the victim's back; his ankles were bruised by a tangle of chain. He looked old, exhausted, further aged by suffering.

Ryre hated slavery as only a man who has been enslaved can. Fury parched his throat. Yet he could not fight a town, nor its customs, however deplorable. He made to ride by, past the corpse of one of the immense almost brainless crawlers of the forest, which must have wormed too close to the swordsmen. Chunks of its flesh had been stripped from the bone; its eye gazed emptily at Ryre from the centre of the lolling head. The slaves must have eaten the flesh raw.

The standing man grew tired of kicking his victim. He said loudly "I'm wasting my strength. You're past your usefulness. Tonight you'll ride above the trees."

The effect of his words was immediate and dismaying. His victim soiled himself in terror. The other slaves glanced upward, and shuddered; Ryre heard a distant flapping. All at once unable to bear his inability to intervene, he urged his steed to canter.

But the slave-driver had seen his glare of contempt. "Yes, ride on, unless you're seeking honest toil. We've a place for you, and chains to fit." His slow voice was viciously caressing as a whip. As he gazed up at Ryre, he licked his lips.

Ryre's grin was leisurely and mirthless. Though he could not battle slavery, he would enjoy responding to this challenge. He stared at the man as though peering beneath a stone. "Ridding the world of vermin? Yes, I'd call that honest."

The man's tongue flickered like a snake's. His smile twitched, as did his hand: nervous, or beckoning for reinforcements? "What kind of swordsman is it who lets his words fight for him?" he demanded harshly.

"No man fights with vermin. He crushes them."

Swordsmen were advancing stealthily. "Perhaps his words are a sheath to keep his sword from rusting," one said. Let them think Ryre's awareness was held by the duel of words. He would cut down his challenger when he was ready, together with anyone else who dared attack him. Unhurriedly he withdrew his sword from its sheath.

A third man spoke, drawing Ryre's attention to the far tip of the advancing crescent of men. "He'll wear our bracelet well."

His steed's uneasy movement warned Ryre. He glanced back in time to see why they were trying to distract him: a man was creeping carefully over the decayed leaves, ready to drag Ryre down and club him with a sword-hilt.

Discovered, the man leapt back—but not swiftly enough. The quick slash of Ryre's blade failed to cleave his skull; instead, the sword bit lower. The man staggered away moaning, trying to hold his cheek to his face.

The others rushed at Ryre. When the original challenger flinched back from the whooping arc of the sword, however, they retreated too. The man seemed wary not only of Ryre but also of the darkening sky. "Let him go," he snarled, trying to sound undaunted. "We've no time to waste on him—not now."

The drivers tugged the chains. It was clearly a signal, for the chains drew loudly taut and dragged their victims into the town like strings of struggling fish. Ryre saw the old man stumbling to keep up. The slaves were pulled staggering into a large wooden barn, which resounded with an uproar of metal links. The great doors thudded shut.

The sight infuriated Ryre. He was scarcely heartened by the agony of the slave-driver, clutching his face as companions aided him into a structure like a barracks next to the barn. Shrugging beneath the weight of his frustration, Ryre rode into the port of Gaxanoi.

In the streets men were lighting lamps. Flames fluttered in vases of thick glass which dangled from poles sprouting next to the central gutters. The entire small town was built of wood; the dim narrow streets reminded him of the forest. But at least a chill salt wind blew through the town, which creaked like an enormous ship. Above the forest the flapping was louder.

Like the streets, the dockside was almost deserted. Ryre's mounted shadow accompanied him, jerking hugely over logs that formed walls. Seamen were entering taverns beside the wharf. On the dock, next to a lone ship, timber lay waiting to be loaded in trade for, among other commodities, chains. He grinned sourly. Gaxanoi had summed itself up.

Eventually he found the harbour-master's house, over-looking the wharf. The man proved reluctant to open his door, and taciturn when he did so. At last he admitted grudgingly that there might be ships tomorrow on which Ryre could work his passage. "Stay near the wharf," he advised, already closing the door.

Ryre did so, in a tavern, once he had stabled his steed nearby. The streets resembled decks of a ship of the dead. The only sounds of life were the clatter and panting of a boy who ran from tavern to tavern, apparently bearing a message. As Ryre entered the tavern the boy ran out, flinching wild-eyed from him.

A few sailors sat on benches, drinking morosely. Each stared into the steady flame in the glass vase before him. Frequently one or other of them would glance up like a wary beast. They seemed to resent having to spend a night in Gaxanoi—or, Ryre suspected, this particular night. He wished he knew more about the town than its name.

Was it their resentment that made the seamen dangerous? One demanded of the taverner why the door was unlocked. When his companions tried to restrain him he fought savagely; the floorboards made it sound like giants were wrestling. The fight spilled out of the tavern, and Ryre observed that the sailors quickly stunned the drunken man and dragged him hastily inside.

"What is out there?" Ryre asked one—but the man glared, seeming almost to blame him for the fracas. When Ryre asked the question of the taverner, he shook his head nervously. "Nothing that I care to speak of."

Ryre had his wooden tankard refilled, and sat by a window. Let whatever was abroad in the night stay out there—but he wasn't about to blind himself with drink and glassed flame: if a threat was approaching, he meant to see it before it came too near.

Still, there seemed to be little to see. Beside the ship, vases flickered on their poles. Waves lapped sleepily at the dock; light snaked in the water. A thin chill wind swung the vases. Shadows of poles danced, advancing, retreating. The ship rocked; it creaked, muffled and monotonous. Ryre shook himself free of its wooden lullaby—for suddenly there was something to watch.

At first he could hardly make out the swimming shapes below the far end of the wharf: a pack of white rats, advancing through black water? Then the vases swayed, and showed him the figures whose cowled heads he'd glimpsed reflected in the sea.

Their robes were pale as fungus. They emerged two by two from a wide dark street at the edge of the dock. The slow pallid emergence reminded Ryre of worms dropping from a gap. There seemed no end to the procession; surely it would fill the wharf.

Despite its size, the procession was unnervingly silent. A distant flapping could be heard. But there was violence amid the ceremony: figures struggling desperately but mutely, which seemed to hover in the air among their robed captors. Ryre distinguished that the victims were bound and gagged, and kept aloft by taut ropes held by robed men. The sight made him think of insects in a web.

As the vanguard came abreast of the window, Ryre saw that the first victim was the slave whom he had seen struck down. The old man looked too exhausted to struggle; he hung slack in the air—but his eyes were lurid with terror. The procession halted as though to display him. A seaman muttered nervously "What do they want?"

At once Ryre knew, and sprang to his feet, cursing. He drew his sword as the tavern door crashed open. Six hooded men came in, swift and silent as predators. Only their robes whispered, and glimmered like marshlight in the dimness. One man pointed at Ryre, and his companions imitated him. The foremost and tallest intoned "He is to fly."

His voice was low, yet seemed as massive as the creaking which had caged Ryre in the forest. No doubt his ritual words terrified slaves, and perhaps the whole of Gaxanoi. But to Ryre the six were only men who had to hide their faces in cowls—and one of them, the man who had pointed him out and whose cowl now sagged back treacherously, was the slave-driver who had challenged him.

The high priest—presumably the tall man called himself something of the kind—stood aside. Three men stepped forward; swords sneaked from beneath their robes. The slave-driver and another man hung back, ready with ropes to bind their victim.

One swordsman advanced, while his companions began to circle their prey. They meant to trap Ryre in the cramped maze of tables and benches, which were fastened securely to the floor. But the furniture helped Ryre. He leapt backward onto a bench; then, as his adversary lunged at him, sprang onto the bench behind the man. Before the swordsman could react, a blow of Ryre's sword had split his skull. He sprawled over a table, his head spilling like an overturned tankard of blood.

Ryre leapt from table to table, heading for the door. Wood thundered around him. As he reached the door, the priest retreated hastily along the wall. One stroke of the blade severed the web of ropes—but four men came running from the procession, swords gleaming eagerly.

Could Ryre hold the priest hostage? Perhaps—but as he made to seize the man, a blade came hissing toward Ryre's neck. Only a desperate leap sideways saved him from the blow, which bit deep into a log of the wall. He whirled; his movement added force to his blade's sweep. The second swordsman crumpled, bowing his half-severed head.

Ryre had been driven back into the tavern. He stared about wildly. The seamen had withdrawn into the shadows, and clearly wanted no part of the fight; the same appeared true of the taverner. Beyond the vats of wine, Ryre glimpsed a rough staircase. If he reached an upper window, he could escape through the alley—if it was unguarded.

He dodged backward between the tables. His scything blade cleared a space around him. By the time the swordsmen saw his plan, and rushed toward the stairs, Ryre was nearly at the vats. As he reached them, the taverner grabbed a heavy wooden scoop from beside a vat. Before Ryre could turn, the taverner had clubbed him down.

The swordsmen were on Ryre at once. One knocked the sword from his hand, another inserted the point of his blade beneath Ryre's chin to lever him to his feet. "Come," he said with cruel tenderness. "They are hungry. Can't you hear them?"

Ryre heard only the taverner's fearful muttering. "Take him out. I got him for you. Take him out and let me lock the doors."

Belatedly Ryre understood why the boy had been running from tavern to tavern. He turned on the taverner, snarling—but at once four sword-points pricked his neck. The points, a lethal collar, urged him out onto the wharf.

The procession and the bared swords closed around him. His captors unbelted their robes, which they had gathered up in order to pursue him. The gliding robes helped muffle the advance of the procession. Ryre was silent too: not from awe, but because all his being was alert for a chance to make his escape.

If he so much as moved his head to ease his cramped neck, a sword-point drew his blood. At least they had been unable to remove his armour, whose leaves would simply tighten about him unless he first relaxed. He trudged onward, a puppet strung by its neck. Vases swung their lights, and made the town sway. Houses floated by, rocking with shadow, locking up fear. The flapping was closer, and sounded impatient.

Soon they entered the forest. At the edge of the town, robed men had seized vases; the light groped amid the gigantic leaves, or wandered away vaguely into the reaches of the forest. This was not the road which Ryre had followed, and which he had assumed to be the sole track. Where did this road lead, and to what evil purpose?

The multitude of trees rose above him. They glistened like pillars of a submerged temple, secret and threatening. Smells of warm luxuriance and decay oppressed him. Huge dim leaves twitched as stored rain fell; the dark dripping avenues sounded like an infinity of moist caves. Somewhere was a leathery fluttering, sluggish and restless. Once he had heard such a clamour deep in a cave that stank of beasts and blood.

Far down the leafy tunnel the dimness was shifting. It fluttered pallidly. Ahead the leathery restlessness grew louder, peremptory. Sword-points bit into Ryre's neck. Were his captors ensuring that he could not escape, or making him the scapegoat of their own fears?

They prodded him forward into the open. As he stumbled from beneath the trees, he saw that the pale stirring was only of moonlight and shade. The moon had risen above distant forested mountains, and showed him a wide glade, bare except for unstable shadows. Above the trees hovered a host of dry eager flapping.

Ryre felt a sword reach for his jugular vein. He tensed: if he was to die here, he'd leave a few agonizing memories among his captors. But the sword relaxed as the slave-driver said gloating "Save him for last. Let him watch."

The trussed victims were carried into the glade. Ryre saw how hastily they were dropped, and how the robed men scurried out of the glade, glancing fearfully at the sky. Despite the size of the procession, there were only four victims. One did not struggle—because he was already dead, Ryre saw; he looked days dead. Presumably this rite served as funeral in Gaxanoi.

All at once the flapping was violent above the glade. Ryre could not lift his head to see, but he glimpsed nightmare shadows roaming over the ground. "Now," the slave-driver hissed.

As swords rose to tap his veins, Ryre sprang. He had slumped a little, bending his knees, as though crushed by despair. Now he leapt to his full height, a head taller than any of them, and launched himself at the slave-driver. Sword-points ripped tracks down his neck—but his shoulders knocked two blades aside, while the others thudded against his armour, bruising his torso. Before the man's exultant grin had time to collapse into panic, Ryre had smashed his fist into the slave-driver's face.

The man staggered backward into the glade, flailing the air with his sword, and fell. But the shock failed to jar the hilt from his grasp. Ryre rushed at him to grapple for the weapon. The sword sprang up. Had Ryre not dodged aside, he would have been emasculated.

The hooded men hung back, daunted by the flapping. How much time had Ryre to gain himself a weapon? The sound of great dry wings descended; shadows swallowed the glade. As he circled the prone man, staying just out of reach of the sweeps of the sword while he tried to dizzy his victim, Ryre glanced up—and gasped, appalled.

Flapping down from the pale sky, in a flock which stank of caverns and worse, came wings. Their span was greater than the spread of his arms. They were the blotchy white of decay; between their bony fingers, skin fluttered lethargically as drowned sails. All this was frightful—but there was no body to speak of between each pair of wings, only a whitish rope of flesh thin as a child's arm. Yet as a pair of wings sailed down near him, Ryre saw a mouth gape along the whole length of the scrawny object. Its lips resembled a split in fungus, and it was crammed with teeth.

The slave-driver scrabbled backward toward the trees, mumbling in terror. One pair of wings settled on a bound victim, like a carelessly flung shroud; then they rose, lifting their prey toward the moon. Ryre's spirit sickened, for the mouth was embedded in the length of the man's chest. The lips worked, sucking.

Enraged and dismayed, Ryre forced his adversary away from the trees. But neither could Ryre flee that way, for the shade bristled with swords. The man twisted on the ground, moaning—then made a vicious lunge with his sword. It was too violent. It hurled the sword from his grip, to impale the ground beside Ryre.

Ryre seized the hilt. Now he could defend himself as best he might, though the weapon was less well-balanced than his own, and heavier. He heard the thud of another sword, thrown to his adversary. The watchers barred the way into the forest. They intended the man to finish Ryre, rather than risk combat themselves.

24

Somewhere behind him, far too numerous and close, Ryre heard wings. They would be enough to contend with when he tried to cross the glade. Before the slave-driver could reach the thrown sword, a slash of Ryre's blade hamstrung him.

Ryre was turning, ready to dash for the far side of the glade, when a shadow engulfed the earth around him. He had no time to react before he was flung to the ground. Once, on board ship, he had been crushed by a fallen sail. He was as helpless now—but this burden felt as though it had been dragged from a swamp. A stench as of something dead and disinterred filled his nostrils. Though he had clung to the sword, his sword-arm was pinned down, useless. He could only snarl and writhe impotently as teeth bit through his armour and fastened in his back, beside his spine.

He felt the lips tear his armour like paper, widening the gap. He lay in wait, and forced himself to suffer the sucking of the mouth embedded in his flesh. As soon as the wings lifted him, he began to chop at the nearest. But they were tougher than his armour. The sword hardly marked them.

He was being lifted, as he might have caught up an infant. The glade whirled away below him; the forest was a moonlit whirlpool, dizzying. He felt himself dangling from teeth clenched deep in his flesh. He hacked at the wings, haphazardly and frenziedly—until he felt the sword grow heavier. The feaster was draining his strength with his blood.

The shrieks of the slave-driver afforded Ryre grim satis-faction. He saw the man borne upward struggling by avid wings. But the sight dwindled; Ryre's wings were carrying him above the trees. He hurled himself about, trying to force the wings toward the leaves, to entangle them. But he could not control their flight; he was merely wasting his strength.

The forest plummeted below him. Deafening winds grabbed his breath. A chill seized him—because of the giddy height, or the leathery fans of wings, or the ebbing of his vitality? The swaying moon steadied; it seemed unnaturally close, perhaps because the wings crowded the sky with its colour.

25

Beneath him, the world consisted of nothing but trees. The shrunken forest drifted by, a dense mosaic formed by countless concentric patterns of leaves. It looked unreal; his sense of perspective was floating away, into something like a dream. Among the flock of wings, a few seed-bearing leaves glided by.

Was the mouth poisoning him as well as drinking his blood? Perhaps, for as his wings swooped higher he was possessed by a kind of insidious delirium. He felt he had sprouted wings which obeyed his dreams. They had transformed him. No longer was he doomed to earthbound plodding. He was a creature of the air, with only the approaching moon, the gliding leaves, the rest of his flock for companions.

A glimpse of that flock pierced his delirium. Around him airborne mouths gaped, hungry for the leavings. His wings lifted him greedily. They were gaining height thanks to his blood, and because he was growing lighter. The other feeding pairs of wings rose exultantly. As their victims turned moon-pale, the gorged wings glowed blotchily pink. Like remains in a web, the victims hardly struggled now.

All at once Ryre saw his chance. The moon swayed like a spider's cocoon shaken by the gusts of the wings; the dwarfed forest looked insubstantial as the blanched sky. Sly waves of vertiginous ecstasy crept over him, blurring his vision further. But he had seen a broad leaf gliding toward him. If it drifted sufficiently close—

It did, and at once was impaled by an upward thrust of his sword. The additional burden had no effect on his headlong flight, but that was not his plan. Instead, he thrust the leaf among the fingertips of one wing, to hinder them. The wing struggled; off balance, the feaster dropped toward the trees—and the leaf ripped, almost wrenching the sword from his grasp. He had to cling to the hilt with both hands to prevent the weapon from falling with the torn leaf.

He grew frenzied. Ramming the sword into his belt, he seized the bony arms of the wings, either to break them or to

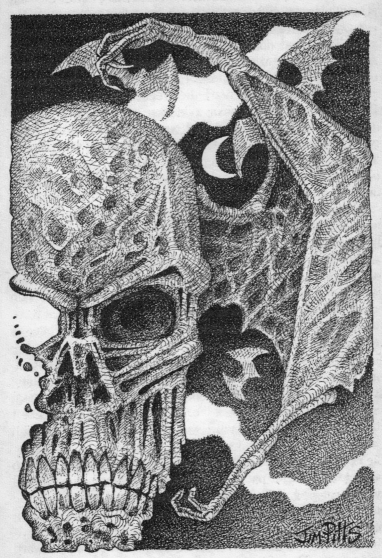

But he preferred a clean death to suffering the humber of the wings.
(Art: Jim Pitts)

wrench the mouth out of his flesh. Why had he waited so long? Though his muscles trembled with his gathered strength, the wings brushed his hands aside. In any case he would achieve only a fall to his death; but he preferred a clean death to suffering the hunger of the wings. Ahead he could see their lair.

It was a blotch of darkness, roughly circular and perhaps a hundred yards wide, among the trees. Wings circled above its rim, like witches dancing a delirious ritual. Was it another glade? As the foremost pair of burdened wings dropped its victim—the bound corpse—into the circle, Ryre saw that the lair was a pit.

His own wings bore him helplessly closer. He glimpsed the depths, and nausea giddied him. He clutched the sword-hilt. Rather than fall conscious into that pit, he would take his own life. Even that ultimate hopelessness was preferable to what waited below.

The rocky sides of the pit were dry. The place resembled the socket of a skull, a desiccated cavity amid the profusion of forest. Its floor was invisible, for the pit was piled with skeletons, tangled indistinguishably. Some of the bones were awesomely gigantic. Atop the pile lay the dropped corpse, as though on a mockery of a pyre.

As Ryre watched aghast, the enormous bony heap stirred. The corpse toppled down its slope. Had the surrounding fecundity possessed the jumble of skeletons, united them into a monstrous parody of life? Ryre's brain whirled, bereft of sense. Then he saw what was crawling out from beneath the bones.

Very slowly and feebly, old wings emerged. They were discoloured as corpses, and looked as though they should have died long ago. A stench of decay welled upward. Dust, no doubt from skeletons, clung to the wings. Their groping reminded him of worms in meat.

They clambered on their fingertips over the bones toward the corpse. They resembled pairs of senile hands, skeletal and webbed. Their lips sagged open, exposing teeth and stumps of teeth. The wings fumbled blindly up the shifting heap; they slid back and clambered again. One by one they reached the corpse and fastened on it. Soon it was entirely covered by a heaving of wings, which divided their victim raggedly and crawled away with their prizes.

Ryre dragged his sword free. The burdened wings hovered above the rim. He knew they were draining their victims before dropping the remnants into the pit. He saw the slave-driver fall, clenched and empty.

The sword felt leaden. Ryre clutched the hilt with his other hand, in case it fell from his enfeebled fingers. Then, snarling at his vindictive fate, he turned the point toward his belly. He meant to drive the blade upwards. Mouths hovered close to him, baring their teeth. He hoped he was weakened enough to die quickly.

Then—though perhaps it would serve only to make his death more ironic—he glimpsed his chance. Was it worth trying? Might he not use up his strength, and be unable even to die cleanly? But he refused to die while he yet had a chance to fight. Without warning he lunged with the sword at the nearest pair of empty wings, and stabbed at the mouth.

He felt the sword pierce flesh within the lips. Yes, the flesh was vulnerable there! He dug the blade deeper, embedding it—and the hilt was almost torn from his hands as the wings flapped convulsively. He managed to keep hold, though his agonized fingers were audibly straining. The hilt was his last hold on life.

Then, as he had prayed inarticulately might happen, the wounded wings became entangled with his own. The leathery struggle caged him; he choked on gusts of decay. He was falling amid the tangle of wings. But as he glimpsed the landscape he roared, enraged by the taunts of his fate. He was falling straight into the pit.

His rage twisted the sword deep in the flesh of the mouth. He heard and felt teeth grind on the blade; he clung grimly to the flailing hilt. The uninjured mouth writhed in his own flesh.

29

For a moment the struggling wings disengaged. He was borne upward, over the rim of the pit.

A few trees sailed by, close enough to grab. But they were withered, and might break. In any case, he dared not let go of the sword. He soared away from the pit, above the denser forest. His strength was still dwindling; the hilt shifted dangerously in his hands. He had no time to choose his moment. Closer to the pit than he would have wished, he dragged the blade toward him with all his remaining force, and entangled the wings.

Convulsed by their struggles, the hilt smashed against his fingers, bruising them. He felt his back tear as the embedded teeth gnashed. But the wings had ensnared one another, and were falling toward the trees.

They crashed through leaves. Cupped rain inundated them. Ryre was deafened by the battle of wings and the ripping of leaves. The trunks grew close here, as though to wall off the aridity of the pit. The wings smashed through another flooded layer, and were caught between trunks. Ryre snarled with gasping mirth as he heard the struggling fingers break.

Still the canopy of leaves gave way. The twitching wings continued to fall. Ryre let go of the sword and embracing a trunk, swung his body with all the violence he could summon. He felt skeletal fingers break. Even then the mouth refused to let go of his flesh. Not until he and the wings had crashed through the lowest leaves to the ground did the teeth part, jarred open by the shock of the fall.

Half-stunned and giddy with the draining, Ryre nonetheless forced himself to his feet. The pairs of wings were hobbling away in the direction of the unseen pit. He wrenched his sword out of the injured mouth and pursued them, stabbing and hacking. But the wings would not die. Though he chopped at the joints of the fingers, and thrust the blade again and again into the mouths, the wings still dragged themselves unevenly toward their lair. Long after he had exhausted the last of his strength and was sitting propped against a tree, with the sword dug into the ground before him to prevent his toppling forward, he heard a ragged flapping and saw pale things crawling lopsidedly away from him, into the dark.

He pressed his back against a drooping leaf, which was cool as balm. His back felt raw, and withered as a mummy's, but seemed to be losing little blood. He dozed, waiting for the dawn and for a hint of his strength to return to him. Nearby there might be leaves whose healing power was greater. He could hear the serpentine denizens of the forest worming their way through the dark arcades. Surely one would be stupid enough to come within reach of his blade. When he could, he would walk—and if his wanderings took him toward Gaxanoi, a few buildings might blaze and a few chains break.

Thomas F. Monteleone

REHEARSALS

Thomas F. Monteleone lives in Baltimore, Maryland, with his wife Linda and son Brandon. Although in his mid-forties he describes himself as "still dashingly handsome". The author of some eighteen novels, including Night Train, The Apocalypse Man, Fantasma, Crooked House, Lyrica *and* The Magnificent Gallery, *his shorter work has been extensively anthologised and can be found in the collections* Dark Stars and Other Illuminations *and* Fearful Symmetries. *He is also editor of the acclaimed horror anthology series* Borderlands. *Tom has written several teleplays, including* Mister Magister *which won the Gabriel Award and the Bronze Award at the International Film and Television Festival in New York. 'Rehearsals' marks the author's first appearance in* Fantasy Tales *and is a poignant tale that blurs the line between fantasy and reality.*

Dominic Kazan walked through the darkness, convinced he was not alone.

The idea cut through him like a razor as he fumbled for the light switch. Where was the damned thing? A sense of panic rose in him like a hot column of vomit in his throat, but he fought it down as his fingers tripped across the switch. Abruptly, the lobby took shape in the dim light.

It, like the rest of the Barclay Theatre, was deserted. Crowds, actors, stagehands—everyone except for Dominic—had left hours ago. And he knew he *should* be alone.

He was the janitor/nightwatchman for the Barclay, accustomed to, and actually comfortable with, the solitude. But for the last few nights, he could not escape the sensation there was something else lurking in the darkness of the big building. Something that seemed to be waiting for him.

He enjoyed working alone; he had been alone most of his life. He did not mind working in almost total darkness; he had lived in a different kind of darkness most of his life.

But this feeling that he was not alone was beginning to bother him, actually frighten him. And he didn't want to have any bad feelings about the Barclay. It was his only true home, and he loved his job there. There was something special about being intimate with the magic of the theatre—the props and costumes, the make-believe world of sets and flats. Sometimes he would come to work early, just to watch the hive-like activity of the stage-hands and actors, feeling the magic-world come to life.

All his life, there seemed to be something stalking him. A mindless kind of thing, a thing of failure and despair. Somehow, it always caught up with him, and threw his life into chaos. He wondered if it was on his trail again.

Tonight. Trying to make him run away again.

And he was so tired, tired of running away . . .

. . . Away from the fragile dreams of his childhood, the traumas of adolescence, and the failures of manhood. His father used to tell him there were only two kind of people in the world: Winners and Losers—and his son was definitely in the second group.

Twenty-eight years old, and it looked like the old man had been right. His life already a worn-out patchquilt of pain and defeat. After pulling a stint in the Army, he had drifted all over the country taking any unskilled job he could find. Seasonal,

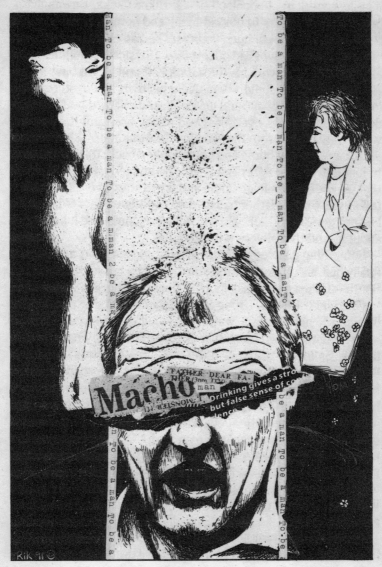

His father looked at him with a hardness, unaffected by the glaze in his eyes. (Art: R. Rawling)

mindless work in Lubbock oil-fields, Biloxi docks, Birmingham factories. Ten years of nomad-living and nomad-losing.

When he had been much younger, he had tried to figure out why things never worked out for him. Physically, Dominic was almost handsome with his thick dark hair and bright blue eyes. And mentally, he could always hold his own. He used to read lots of comics and books and never missed a Saturday afternoon double-feature. He even watched a play now and then, back when they used to run them on live television.

But after he left home and never looked back, things seemed to just get worse. After ten years, he started getting the idea that maybe he should go home and try to start over. The letter telling him that his father had died was now five years old, and he had not gone back then. He had not even contacted his mother about it, and that always bothered him.

Something gnawed at his memories and his guilt, and he had finally quit his rigging job and started hitching East through the South—Louisiana, Mississippi, Alabama, Georgia.

One night, he was sitting in a roadhouse outside of Atlanta, drinking Schlitz on tap, watching a well-dressed guy next to him trying to drown himself in dry martinis. They had started talking, as lonely drinkers often will. The guy was obviously successful, middle-aged, and out-of-place in the roadside bar.

At one point, Dominic had mentioned that he was going home, back to the city of his birth. The stylish man laughed and slurred something about Thomas Wolfe. When Dominic questioned the response, the man said, "Don't you remember him? He's the guy who said, 'you can't go home again,' and then he wrote a long, god-awful boring book to prove it."

Dominic never understood what the man was talking about until he reached his hometown. It was a large East coast city, and it had changed drastically in his absence. Lots of remembered landmarks had vanished; the streets seemed cold, alien. For several days, he gathered the courage to return to his old neighbourhood, to face his mother after so many years.

When he was finally ready, arriving at the correct street, the correct address, he found his house was *gone*.

The entire street, which had once been a cramped, stifling heap of tenements, row houses, and basement shops, had been wiped out of existence. Urban renewal had invaded the neighbourhood, grinding into dust all the bricks and mortar, all the memories.

In its place stood a monstrous building—a monolith of glass and steel and shaped concrete called the Barclay Theatre. At first he saw it as an intruder, a silent, hulking thing which had utterly destroyed his past, occupying the space where his little house had once stood. Perhaps Thomas Wolfe knew what he was talking about.

But after thinking about it, he thought it was ironic that it was, of all things, a theatre that wiped out his memories.

Ironic indeed.

In the days that followed, he tried to locate his mother, but with no success. She had vanished, and a part of him was glad. It would have been difficult to face her as a man with no future, and now, not even a past. For no good reason, he decided to stay on in the city, taking day-labour jobs and a room at the YMCA.

As Dominic drifted into summer, he had made no friends, had not found a steady job, and had given up finding his mother. He read books from the library, went to matinée movies, and lived alone with his broken dreams. Occasionally he would walk back to his old neighbourhood, as though hoping to see his house one final time. And on each visit, he would stand in the light-pool of a street lamp to stare at the elegant presence of the Barclay.

He seemed to feel an attraction to the place, old dreams stirring in a locked room of his mind. One day, when he saw an ad in the paper for a janitor/nightwatchman at the theatre, he ran all the way to apply.

They hired him on a probational basis, but Dominic didn't mind the qualification. He made a point of being on time and very meticulous in his work. As the weeks passed, he felt a growing warmth in his heart for the Barclay; it became a haven of safety and security—a place where he could live with the old dreams.

When his diligence was rewarded with a permanent position and a raise in salary, he was very happy. He began coming early to watch current productions, and he learned the theatre jargon of the stagehands, actors, and directors. The dreamscapes of the theatre became real to him, and he absorbed the great tragedies, laughed at clever comedies.

But late at night, when the crowds had dispersed, was the time he loved the best. He would go into the main auditorium and listen to the lights cooling and crackling behind their gels, and think about that night's performance—comparing to past nights, to what he figured were the playwright's intentions. For the first time in his life, he was happy.

But then something changed. The feelings of not being alone started to grow out of the shadows, growing more intense . . .

. . . until tonight, and he felt that he could bear it no longer. There was a small voice in his mind telling him to run from the place and never return.

No, he thought calmly. No more running. Not ever again.

Above his head, the cantilevered balcony hung like a giant hammer ready to fall. He stepped into the main auditorium and listened to the darkness. The aisle swept down towards the stage where the grand drape and act curtain pulled back to reveal the set of the current play. Pushing a carpet sweeper slowly over the thick pile, Dominic noticed how truly dark the theatre was. The exit light seemed dim and distant. Row upon row of seats surrounded him, like a herd of round-shouldered creatures huddled in deep shadows.

The entire theatre seemed to be enclosing him like an immense vault, a dark hollow tomb. He knew there was something there with him. Acid boiled in his stomach, his throat caked with chalk.

Looking away from the empty seats back to the stage, he noticed that something had changed. Something was wrong.

The set for the currently running production was Nick's Place—a San Francisco saloon described in Saroyan's *The Time of Your Life*. But that set was gone. Somehow, it had been struck, and changed overnight. An impossibility, Dominic knew, yet he stared into the darkness and could make out the configurations of a totally different set.

Walking closer, his eyes adjusting to the dim illumination of the Exit signs, Dominic picked up the details of the set—a shabby, grey-walled living room with a kitchenette to the right. Dumpy green chairs with doilies on the arms, a couch with maroon and silver stripes, end-tables with glass tops and a mahogany liquor cabinet with a tiny-screened Emerson television on top. It was a spare, simple room.

A familiar room.

For an instant, Dominic recoiled at the thought. It couldn't be. It wasn't possible.

But he recognized the room, down to its smallest details. As if the set designer had invaded a private memory, the set was a perfect replica of his parents' house. The house which had been located where the theatre now stood. As Dominic stared in awe and disbelief, he could see that there was nothing dreamy and out-of-focus about the set. He stood before something with hard edges and substance, something real, and not distorted by the lens of memory.

Without thinking, he stepped closer and suddenly the stagelights heated up. The fixtures on the set cast off their greyish hues and burst into full colour. An odd swelling sensation filled Dominic's chest, almost becoming a distinct pain. The pain of many years and many emotions. The thought occurred to him that someone might be playing a very cruel joke on him and he turned to check the light booth up above and beyond the balcony. But it was dark and empty.

The sound of a door opening jarred him.

Turning back to the stage he saw a woman wearing a turquoise housedress and beige slippers enter the room from stage left. She had a roundish face going towards plump and her eyes were flat and lacklustre. There was an essential weariness about her.

Dominic felt tears growing in his eyes, a tightness in his throat, as he looked, stunned, at his mother.

"Mom! Mom, what're you doing here? Hey, Mom!"

But she did not hear him. Mechanically, his mother began setting a simple table with paper napkins, Melmac plates, and plain utensils. Dominic ran up to the edge of the stage and yelled at her but she ignored him. It became clear that she could neither see nor hear him—as though they were dimensions apart, as though he saw everything through a one-way mirror.

What the hell was going on?

Dominic grappled with the sheer insanity of it all, trying to make sense out of the hallucinated moment, when it continued. The door at stage centre flew open and his father entered the set.

At the sight of the man, something tightened around Dominic's heart like a fist, staggering him. His father was dead. And yet, there he was, standing in the doorway full of sweat and shine and dirt. There was a defiance in the old man's posture, in the way he slammed the door shut behind him. He wore greasy chino pants and a plaid flannel shirt. One hand carried a beat-up lunch pail with the word "Kazan" stenciled on the side; the other the evening paper.

Dropping the lunch bucket on the kitchen table, his father moved quickly to his favourite chair and unflapped the paper. If he had acknowledged the presence of his wife, Dominic had missed it. There was a somehow surreal quality to the scene—suggesting more than was actually taking place. He sensed this moment could have been taking place at any point in their lives over perhaps a twenty-year span.

Dominic fought off the emotional waves which crashed over him, trying to concentrate on the images on the stage. He was surprised to see how plain his mother actually was—not the pretty woman of his memories—and how much smaller and less imposing his father seemed. Again the lens of memory had worked its distorted magic.

The door at stage left abruptly opened and a small, frightfully thin boy of perhaps nine years entered the room. The boy had large ears, bright blue eyes, and Brylcream-slicked dark hair. Dominic felt stunned as he recognized the boy as himself. He had never realized how frail and odd he had looked as a child; he winced as he heard the young boy speak in a high-pitched voice.

> BOY
>> Hi, Daddy!

The boy advanced to his father's chair, carrying a sheaf of papers.

> BOY
>> Look what me and Beezie are goin' to do . . . !

The greeting was met with silence. His father's face remained hidden behind the newspaper.

> MOTHER
>> Joseph, the boy is talkin' to you.

> FATHER
>> Eh! What does he want?!

The paper dropped to the working man's lap, and the father stared at his son with a slack, almost hostile expression.

BOY

Daddy, look! Beezie and me
are goin' to direct a play! And
we're goin' to charge ten cents
apiece for all the kids to come
and see it.

(hands some papers to his
father)
Here's some drawings I made
. . . See, this is Snow White's
house, and—

FATHER

Play? *Snow White*? That's a
fairy tale, ain't it?

BOY

Yeah, it's like the Walt Disney
movie, and—

The father laughed roughly.

FATHER

A fairy tale is for a buncha
fairies!
(he sweeps out his hand,
scattering the drawings
across the floor)
That's nothin' for a boy to be
up to! Plays are for fairies . . .
you want to be a *fairy*, boy?

BOY

But, Daddy, it's a good show,
and—

FATHER

>Listen, pick up this crap and get it outta here. And don't let me hear no more about it. You oughta be out playin' ball . . . not foolin' with this pansy crap!

Dominic stood in the aisle, his mind reeling from the impact of the scene. How he remembered that night! His father had so thoroughly crushed him that evening that he had given up the play with his friend. He had let a little piece of himself die that night.

A sudden anger surged through him as he forced his mind back to the rest of the memory, and he remembered what happened when he had started picking up his drawings.

Up on the stage, his younger self was bending down, reaching out for the scattered papers.

Stepping closer to the stage, Dominic cried out. "Watch it! Don't let him get to them first . . . he's going to tear them up!"

The skinny, dark-haired boy paused, looked out into the darkness of the audience, as though listening. His mother and father had clearly heard nothing, and for a moment, seemed to be arrested in time.

BOY

>(looking down towards Dominic)
>What did you say?

"Dad's going to tear up your drawings . . . if you let him," said Dominic. "So pick them up now, fast. Then tell him what you're thinking, what you're feeling."

> BOY
>> Who are you?

    Dominic swallowed hard, forced himself to speak in a clear, calm voice. "You know who I am . . ."

> BOY (smiling)
>> Yeah, I guess I do . . .

The boy turned back to the stage and quickly grabbed all his drawings as his father reached down a large hand and tried to snatch them away.

> BOY
>> No! You leave them alone!
>> You leave me alone!

> FATHER
>> (a bit shocked by the boy's words)
>> What're ya gonna do?
>> Grow up and be a fruitcake?
>> Whatsamatter with baseball?
>> Too tough on ya?

The boy held the papers to his chest, paused to look out into the darkness at Dominic, then back to his father. The boy was breathing hard, obviously scared, but there was a new strength in the way he stood, staring at his father. He was almost sobbing, but he forced the words to come out clearly.

> BOY
>> Yeah, I like baseball just fine.
>> But I like this stuff, too. And
>> . . . and, I don't care if you

don't like it. Cause I do! And
that's what's important!

The boy ran from the room, carrying his drawings. His father
stared after him for a moment, then returned to his newspaper,
trying to act unaffected by the small exchange. His mother
stood by the table with a beaten, joyless expression on her face.

The stage lights dimmed quickly, fading everything into
darkness. Dominic blinked his eyes as the figures of his parents
became phantoms in the shadows, growing faint, insubstantial.
Another blink of his eyes and they were gone. Slowly the set
began to metamorphose back into the barroom of Nick's Place.
Dominic's heart cried out silently, but it was too late. The
vision, or whatever it had been, had vanished.

He took an aisle seat, let out a long breath. Rubbing his eyes,
he felt the fine patina of sweat on his face. His heartbeats were
loud and heavy. What the hell had been going on? He had been
awake, yet he felt as though he had just snapped out of a trance.
He felt crazy, but he knew that he was not dreaming, not unless
his whole life had been a nightmare.

It had seemed so real. How obvious the dynamics of his family
seemed to him now. He wondered why he had never seen what
things were really like when he was a kid. But then, maybe he
did know back then . . .

Children picked up things on a different level than adults.
They hadn't spent much time building up defense mechanisms
and rationalizations for all the shitty things that happen in the
world. Kids take everything straight, no chaser. It's later on
we all start bullshitting ourselves.

Dominic stood up and looked about the auditorium as an eerie
sensation washed over him. It was as though he was the only
person left in the whole world. He felt so totally alone. And he
knew that it was time to get away from this place. Try to forget
all the pain—isn't that what life is all about?—not wallow in it.

He walked back to the lobby, slipped through a side door,
and then down a long corridor to his office. After turning out

the lights, he locked up, headed for the employee's exit. Just as he reached the fire door, he heard footsteps in the shadows behind him. He whirled quickly and saw a small, hunched-over black man carrying a broom.

"Evenin', Mr. Kazan . . ." said the voice.

"Oh hi, Sam," said Dominic. "Take it easy now. Goodnight." He pushed out the door to the parking lot, leaving the old janitor/nightwatchman alone in the building.

The next day when Dominic Kazan awoke, he felt somehow changed, but there was nothing he could think of which would explain the feeling. He had no memory of the previous night's experience, other than a nagging question in his mind. It was a crazy idea he must have been dreaming about, but there was something he wanted to know.

That afternoon, before going down to the Barclay, Dominic stopped at City Office Building to speak to some people in the records division of the Department of Urban Planning. They were as cooperative as bureaucrats can be, and after more than two hours of hassling around, Dominic chanced upon a few intriguing facts.

In the theatre that evening after the performance, Dominic went about his duties. As stage manager, he had to make certain that all the props were back in place for the next show, that the set was restored to pre-curtain readiness, and that all the light and sound cues were in the proper order in the technician's booth. He went through his tasks slowly, waiting for the rest of the Barclay personnel to depart the large building.

Entering the main auditorium, Dominic walked down the aisle and sat in the first row of the orchestra seats. A silence pervaded the place as he closed his eyes, letting his thoughts run free. His discovery at the Department of Urban Planning kept replaying in his mind—the proscenium stage of the Barclay occupied the very same space that was once filled by his parents' house in the middle of the old neighbourhood block.

Dominic opened his eyes slowly, focusing on the stage. As though on cue, the lights heated up, gradually filling the set with hard illumination. But this time, he did feel fear as much as anticipation. He felt like he was about to embark upon a long-awaited trip.

Dominic looked up to see his familiar living room warming under the stage lights.

The door opened and his father entered the room. He wore his usual work clothes, carried an evening paper and his lunch pail. Normally a quick-moving, broadly-shouldered man who seemed to radiate force and raw power, Joseph Kazan appeared stooped and oddly defeated.

FATHER
Louisa! Louisa, where are you?!

There was no immediate reply and he shrugged as he moved to his favourite chair. He began to open his folded newspaper, then threw it to the floor in disgust. A door opened at stage left and Dominic's mother appeared carrying a dish towel.

MOTHER
Joseph? What are you doing home so early?

Joseph looked at her with anger in his eyes, his lips curled back slightly. Suddenly the anger drained away from him. Looking away from his wife, he spoke with great effort.

FATHER
We got laid off again today . . . Got mad at my foreman. I left after he told us all not to come in tomorrow morning.

47

There was a pained expression in his mother's face.

> **MOTHER**
> Why do they always do this right before Christmas? It's not fair.

> **FATHER**
> I'll have to find somethin' quick. We got bills to keep up. Nobody's hirin' now, though . . . the bastards!

His mother moved to his father's chair, put a hand on his shoulder.

> **MOTHER**
> Well, we've gotten by before . . . we'll do it again.

Joseph shook his head, slapped his leg absently.

> **FATHER**
> Some husband I been! A man's spozed to take care of things! Take care of his family better'n this!

The door at stage centre opened and an adolescent version of Dominic entered the room. He was carrying a stack of books under his arm, his parka under the other.

> **BOY**
> Hi Mom . . . hey Dad, what're you doing home early?

FATHER
>(ignoring the question)
>Where you been?

BOY
>We had a rehearsal after
>school. Just got finished.
>(to his mother)
>Can I have an apple or some-
>thing, Mom?

FATHER
>Rehearsal-what? Another one
>of them plays?

BOY
>C'mon Dad, you know I'm
>doing a play for the one-act
>contest at school. I wrote it
>myself, remember?

His father shook his head slowly, wiped his mouth with obvious
irritation, then looked at his mother.

FATHER
>I'm worryin' about takin' care
>of this family, he's out writin'
>stuff for faggots!

His mother touched her husband's shoulder again.

MOTHER
>Joseph, please don't take it
>out on him . . .

> BOY
>> Yeah, Dad. We've been
>> through this stuff before,
>> haven't we?

Dominic's father did not speak as he exploded from his chair
and backhanded the teenager across the face with one quick,
furious motion. The force of the blow slammed the boy's head
against the wall and he staggered away, dazed and glassy-
eyed.

> FATHER   .
>> More! You want more! You
>> smart-assed kid! You don't
>> speak to your father like
>> that . . . not never!

His mother moved to help her wounded son.

> MOTHER
>> You didn't have to hit him like
>> that.

> FATHER
>> You stay away from him,
>> Goddammit! I oughta give
>> it to him twice as hard! He
>> don't respect his father. At
>> his age he oughta be out
>> workin' like a man. He oughta
>> be helpin' his family!

The teenaged boy looked at his father with terror in his eyes.
He appeared helpless, but he forced himself to speak.

                    BOY
                              What do you want from me?
                              What have I ever done to hurt
                              you?

                    FATHER
                                  (in mocking effeminate
                              voice)
                              What have I ever done to hurt
                              you!

His father grinned at his little joke, then raised his hand towards
the boy, just to watch him shy away.

                    FATHER (cont'd)
                              I'll tell you what you done . . .
                              you ain't acted like a man! And
                              that hurts more'n anything.
                              But that's gonna stop. As of
                              today you're gonna be a man.

                    BOY
                              What do you mean?

                    FATHER
                              You're goin' to work.

                    BOY
                              But I already have a job . . .

                    FATHER
                              Ha! You call that paper route
                              a job? I'm talkin' about a
                              real job. Make some real
                              money! It's about time you

                              51

started helpin' your mother and me.

BOY

But what about school?

His father laughed, then stared at him defiantly.

FATHER

What about it? You're old enough to quit . . . so now you'll quit! I hadda leave school in the fifth grade! You think you're any better'n me?

BOY

But Dad, I don't want to quit school. I can't quit now.

FATHER

Don't tell me what you "can't" or what you "want" cause that don't mean shit to me! I'm tellin' you what you gotta do cause I'm your father! That school's just fillin' your head with a bunch of crazy shit anyway . . .

BOY

Dad, I can't believe this . . .

FATHER

Shut-up and listen to me or I'll bust you again!

Dominic had been watching the scene with a morbid fascination and a growing anger. Things seemed so much clearer now—how things worked in his family. He could not allow his younger self to succumb to the ravings of a beaten, humiliated man.

Without thinking further, he stood up and called out to the younger version of himself: "Hey! You tell him to keep his hands off you! And that if he tries anything again . . . you're going to stop him!"

As before, neither his father nor mother seemed to have heard Dominic's voice. But the adolescent boy reacted immediately. He turned to the edge of the stage and peered into the darkness.

> BOY
>> What did you say? Is it you again?

"Yes," said Dominic, his voice almost catching in his throat. "It's me . . . now tell him what I told you. Tell him what you're thinking. What you're really thinking."

Dominic watched the boy nod and turn back towards his father. There was a sensation of great tension in the air, like an electrical storm gathering on a humid day.

> BOY
>> You can't hit me like that anymore.

The boy stood there, seeming to radiate a new strength.

> FATHER
>> What?

> BOY
>> You can't hit me just because you feel like doing it. I haven't

53

done anything wrong and I'm tired of you making me feel like I have.

FATHER
I'll bust you any Goddamned time I—

BOY
No! No you won't! I won't let you!

His father smiled and shifted his weight from one foot to the other, his arms hanging loose as though ready for a fight.

FATHER
Well, what's this? A little manliness after all this time, huh? How about that?

BOY
I'm not quitting school. And you can't make me do it. There're things I want to do with my life that I can't do if I quit school.

His father looked at him silently, a confused expression on his face.

BOY (cont'd)
There're things I want to do ... things that you could never do.

FATHER

What the hell's that spozed to
mean?

BOY

You have to understand
something, Dad. I'm not
going to be made responsible
for anybody's life . . . except
my own. Especially not yours.
I can't live your life, but
I have to live mine.

FATHER (looking confused, off-balance)

Listen, you little shit . . .

BOY

No, Dad, I think it's time
you listened. Maybe for the
first time in your life.

The boy turned and walked to the door stage centre, opening
it.

BOY

I'm going out for awhile.

He exited the stage, leaving his father standing mute and
stripped of his power.

Dominic fell back in the theatre seat as the stage quickly
darkened and the figures and props dissolved into the
shadows. In an instant the set was gone. He felt rigid and
tense and there was a soft roaring in his ears like the sound
of a sea shell. He felt as though he had just awakened from a
dream. But he knew it had been no dream.

A memory?

Perhaps. But as he sat there in the darkness, he had the feeling he had no memories. That the scene he had just witnessed was a solitary moment, a free-floating, always existing piece of the timestream. A moment out of time.

What is *happening* to me? The thought ate through him like a furious acid, leaving him with a vague sense of panic. Standing up, he knew that he must leave the place. Dominic walked up the aisle to the lobby, refusing to look back at the dark stage.

The light in the lobby comforted him and he felt better immediately. Already, the fears and crazy thoughts were fading away. It's all right now. Better get on home. As he moved towards the exit, he heard a sound and stopped. A door slipping its latch.

"Mr. Kazan!" said a familiar voice. "What're you still doing here?"

Turning, Dominic saw Bob Yeager, the Barclay's stage manager, standing in the doorway of his office.

"Oh hi, Bob. I was . . . I was just going over a few things. Just getting ready to leave."

Yeager rubbed his beard, grinned. "Just getting over those first-night jitters, huh? I can understand that, yes sir."

Dominic smiled uneasily. "Yeah, the first night's always the worst . . ."

"Hey, you did a great job, Mr. Kazan. Just fine."

"I did?"

Yeager nodded, smiled.

"I suppose I'll have to take your word for it," said Dominic. "Well, I guess I'd better be heading home. Good night."

When he arrived at his townhouse, he found that he couldn't sleep. He had the nagging sensation that something was wrong, that something in his life was out of whack, out of synch, but he couldn't pin it down. After making a cup of instant coffee, he wandered into his den where a typewriter and a pile of manuscript pages awaited him on a large messy desk.

Sitting down, he decided to go back to that play he had been trying to write. Every actor thinks he can be a playwright, right? Some ideas started flowing as Dominic began to type, and it was very late before he went to bed.

The next evening's performance had gone better than opening night, but it was still rough. Dominic was playing the part of Alan in Wilson's *Lemon Sky*, and although the director was pleased with his characterization, Dominic was not. He had learned long ago that you cannot merely please your audience; you must also please yourself.

He remained in the dressing room, dawdling and taking his time, waiting for everyone else to leave. The rest of the cast planned to meet at their favourite bistro for drinks and food, and he had declined politely. There would be time for such things later. Tonight, Dominic felt compelled to go back into the theatre itself, back into the empty darkness where careers were made or destroyed.

He was not really certain why he felt the need to stay behind. But he had feelings, or rather, memories. Or perhaps they were dreams . . . or memories of dreams.

He was not certain what they were, but he felt convinced that the answers lay in the dark shadows of the auditorium.

Finally, everyone had cleared out and he left the dressing room for the theatre itself. As he entered through the lobby doors, he saw no one, not even Sam. There were no lights, other than the green, glowing letters of the exit lights, and as he moved down the aisle, he had the sensation of entering an abandoned cathedral. The darkness seemed to crowd about him like a thick fog, and he began to feel strangely light-headed. As he drew himself deeper into the vast sea of empty seats, he could see the dim outlines of the set beyond the open act-curtain—a modern suburban home in El Cajon, California.

Then slowly, the stage lights crackled as they gathered heat, and bathed the stage in light and life. The shapes which took form and colour were again the props of a tortured childhood.

The shabby living room, the kitchenette, worn carpets and dingy curtains.

The door at stage centre opened and his mother entered, wearing a simple, tailored suit. Her hair was silvering and had been puffed by a beauty shop. She appeared elegant in a simply stated manner. He had never remembered his mother looking like that. She looked about the room as though expecting someone to be home.

> MOTHER
> Dominic, where are you?
> Dominic?

She appeared perplexed as she closed the door, calling his name again. Then turning towards the footlights, she looked beyond them to where he stood transfixed.

> MOTHER (cont'd)
> Oh there you are. Dominic,
> come up here! Come to
> me . . .

The recognition startled him, but he felt himself responding as though wrapped in the web of a dream. There was an unreality about the moment, a sensation which prompted him to question nothing, to merely react.

And he did.

Climbing up and onto the stage as the heat of the lights warmed him, he felt as though he were passing through a barrier. It was that magic which every actor feels when the curtain rises and he steps forth, but it was also very different this time . . .

> DOMINIC
> Where's Dad? He wasn't
> there, was he?

MOTHER (looking away)
> No, Dominic . . . I'm sorry.
> I don't know where he is.
> He never came home from
> work.

She paused to straighten a doily on the arm of the sofa, then turned back to him.

MOTHER (cont'd)
> But Dominic, it was
> *wonderful*! So beautiful a play,
> I never seen! And *you* were
> wonderful! I am so proud of
> you, my son!

Dominic smiled and walked over to her and hugged her. It was the first time he could remember doing such a thing in a long, long time. Overt affection in his home had been a rarity, something shunned and almost feared.

DOMINIC
> Thanks, Mom.

MOTHER
> I always knew you were a good
> boy. I always knew you would
> make me proud some day.

DOMINIC
> Did you?

He pulled away from her, looked at her intently.

DOMINIC (cont'd)
>Then why didn't you ever
>tell me when I was a kid?
>Back when I really needed
>it.

His mother turned away, stared into the sink.

MOTHER
>You wouldn't understand,
>Dominic. You don't know how
>many times I wanted to say
>something, but . . .

DOMINIC
>But it was him, wasn't it?
>Christ, Mom, were you that
>much afraid of him that you
>could just stand by and watch
>him destroy your only son?

MOTHER
>Don't talk like that, Dominic.
>I prayed for you, Dominic
>. . . I prayed into the night
>that you would be stronger
>than me, that you would
>stand up to him. I did what
>I *could*, Dominic . . .

DOMINIC
>I think I needed more than
>prayers, Mom . . . but that's
>okay. I understand. I'm sorry
>I jumped on you like that.

Then came the sound of a key fumbling in a lock. The click of the doorknob sounded loud and ominous. The door swung open slowly to reveal his father, obviously drunk, leaning against the threshold. Joseph Kazan shambled onto the set, seemingly unaware of anyone else's presence. He collapsed in his usual chair and stared out into empty space.

                    DOMINIC
                         Where have you been?

His father looked at him with a hardness, unaffected by the glaze in his eyes.

                    FATHER
                         What the fuck you care?

                    DOMINIC
                         You're my father. I care.
                         Sons are supposed to care
                         about their fathers . . . or
                         haven't you heard?

                    FATHER (coughing)
                         Don't get wise with me! I
                         can still get out of this chair
                         and whomp you one!

                    DOMINIC (smiling sadly)
                         Is that the only form of com-
                         munication you know?
                         "Whomping" people?

                    FATHER (laughing)
                         Ah, it's not even worth it!
                         You and your fancy words

. . . What do you know about bein' a man?

DOMINIC
Dad, I wanted you to be there tonight. You *knew* I wanted you there . . . didn't you?

His father looked at him and the hardness in his eyes seemed to soften a bit. Looking away, Joseph Kazan spoke in a low voice.

FATHER
Yeah . . . yeah, I knew.

DOMINIC
So why weren't you there? Did it really feel better to crawl into one of those sewers you call a bar and get filthy drunk? Did you think that getting juiced would make it all go away?! What do—

FATHER
Shut up! Shut up before I whomp ya!

His father had put his hands over his ears, trying to shut out the offending words.

DOMINIC
No, I don't think so. I don't think you'll be whomping anybody. Ever again.

FATHER

That's brave words from a
wimp like you.

DOMINIC

Don't talk to me about
"brave." Why didn't you come
to the play tonight? *My* play!
Your *son's* play!

FATHER

What're you talkin' about?

DOMINIC

What were you afraid of,
Dad? That maybe some of
your buddies might see you?
Might catch you going to see
a bunch of "faggots?"

FATHER

Hah! See, you even admit it
yourself!

Dominic's mother moved in between the two men.

MOTHER

Oh God, look at you two! So
much anger . . . so much hate.
Please, stop it . . .

DOMINIC

Hate? No, Mom, that's not
right. A lack of love, maybe
. . . but not really hate.
There's a difference.

FATHER (looking at his son)
>What the hell do you know?

DOMINIC
>I think that's the heart of the problem around here—not enough love in this house. There isn't any love here. No warmth . . . no love.

FATHER
>Shit, I'll tell y'about love! I worked for yer Mom for *thirty-five* years. Worked hard! Did she ever have to go out'n take a job like other guys' wives? Shit, no!

His father was trembling as he spoke, his florid face puffy and shining with sweat.

DOMINIC
>There's more to love than that, Dad. Like the love between you and me . . . When I was a kid, did you ever just sit down and play with me? Did you ever tell me stories, or try to make me laugh? How about going fishing together, or flying a kite? Did we ever do anything like that?

FATHER
>A man has to work!

DOMINIC

Did you really love your work
that much?

FATHER

What do y'mean?

DOMINIC

Did you love your work more
than me?

FATHER (confused, angry)

Don't talk no bullshit to me!

DOMINIC

It's not bullshit, Dad. Listen,
when I was little — no
brothers or sisters — I spent a
lot of time alone. Sometimes I
needed someone to guide me,
to teach me.

FATHER

I never ran out and never
came home at night . . . ask
your mother! I was always
there, every night!

DOMINIC (smiling sadly)

Oh yeah, you were there
physically. But never emo-
tionally, can't you see that?
I can remember seeing other
kids out doing things with

65

their fathers, and I can remember really *hating* them—
because they had something
I never did. That kind of
stuff hurt me a lot more
than your belt ever did.

His father did not respond, but looked down at his lap where
he had unconsciously knotted his hands together.

MOTHER
Dominic, leave him alone now.
Let's all have some coffee, and
we can—

DOMINIC
No, Mom. Let's finish it.
Let's get it all out. It's been
a long time coming.
> (to his father)

Hey, Dad . . . do you know I
have *no* memories of you ever
encouraging me to do *anything? Except all that macho
shit.*

FATHER
What kind of shit?

DOMINIC
Remember when I saved my
paper route money and bought
that cheap guitar?

FATHER
Yeah, so . . .?

DOMINIC

But I guess you've forgotten
how you screamed and yelled
that you couldn't afford music
lessons, and music was only
for "fairies" anyhow?

FATHER

I ain't sure . . .

DOMINIC

Well, *I'm* sure. And when
I told you I'd teach myself
how to play it, you laughed,
remember?

FATHER

Did I?

DOMINIC

Oh yes, and I don't have
to strain to recall how that
felt. It's carved right into my
heart. The whole goddamned
scene.

FATHER

So who ever heard of any-
body teachin' themselves to
play music. It's crazy!

DOMINIC

Yeah, maybe . . . but I *did*
teach myself didn't I? And
I played in a band until

that night I came home late
from a dance and you were
waiting for me behind the
door—Remember that, Dad?
The night you smashed my
guitar over the sink?

His father looked away from him. He seemed truly embarrassed
now.

DOMINIC (cont'd)

That's what my life's been
like, Dad; me doing things
despite what I got from you.
Or maybe I should say what
I didn't get from you!

FATHER

That's horseshit.

DOMINIC (shaking his head)

I wish it was. I really do. But
it's all true, Dad. All true.

FATHER

Why don't you just shut up!

DOMINIC

Because I'm not finished yet.
What's the matter, am I
threatening you? I think that's
what the problem has always
been—you never liked the
way your wide-eyed kid had
some natural curiosity about
the world, did you?

FATHER (sounding tired now)
>You're not making any sense.

DOMINIC
>Well try this one: you weren't only threatened by your son, but just about *everybody*. Anybody you thought was more intelligent than you, or more educated, or had more money . . . you always had something shitty to say about all of them, didn't you?

FATHER
>Now, it ain't like that!

DOMINIC
>Wait! Let me finish. So then you wake up one morning and you realize that your own weirdo kid was not going to grow up to be a beer-drinking macho man, you just gave up, didn't you?

FATHER
>What do you mean?

DOMINIC
>I mean that when you saw that your own kid was turning out to be a hell of a lot different from you—but very much like all those kinds

of peo- ple you feared and
therefore despised— then
you stopped being a father
to that strange son.

FATHER

I what?

DOMINIC

Didn't you know that all I
wanted was a little approval?
A little love?

FATHER

You talk like you got it all
figured out . . . what do you
think you are—a doctor or
something?

DOMINIC (grinning)

No. No "doctor" . . . just a
son. And if I haven't "figured
it all out", at least I'm trying.
You never even tried!

His father stared at him and tried to speak, but no words
would come. His lower lip trembled slightly from the effort.

DOMINIC

Don't you understand why I'm
telling you all this? Don't you
understand what I've been
trying to say?

His father shook his head quickly, uttered a single
word.

                    FATHER
                         No . . .

                    DOMINIC
                         I can't think of anything else
                         to say. No other way to
                         make you understand . . .
                         except to just tell you, Dad.
                         I don't know why, but after
                         all the years, and after all
                         the pain, I know that I still
                         love you, that I have to love
                         you.

He walked closer to his father and stared into his eyes,
searching for some glimmer of understanding.

                    DOMINIC (cont'd)
                         I love you, Dad.
                         (pause)
                         And I need to hear the same
                         thing from you.

There was a long silence as father and son regarded each
other. Dominic could feel the presence of some great force
gathering over the stage. Then he saw the tears forming
in his father's eyes.

                    FATHER (stepping forward)
                         Oh, Dominic . . .

His father grabbed him up in his arms and pulled him close.
For an instant, Dominic resisted, but then relaxed, falling into
the embrace with his father.

Thomas F. Monteleone

FATHER
> My son . . . I *do* love you. I
> . . . I *love* you!

Dominic felt the barrel-chest of his father close against his own and he was very conscious of how strange a sensation it was. Suddenly there was a great roaring in his ears and he was instantly terrified, disoriented. His father had relaxed his emotional embrace and Dominic pulled back and looked into the man's face.

He was only vaguely aware of the stage lights quickly fading to black, but in the last instant of illumination he saw that his father no longer stood before him. He now stared into the face of a stranger.

An actor.

The roaring sound had coalesced into something recognizable, and Dominic turned to look out into the brimming audience—a sea of people who were on their feet, clamouring, applauding wildly. Then the curtain closed, sealing him off from them, from the torrent of appreciation.

He was only half aware of his two fellow actors—the ones who had portrayed his father and mother—as they moved to each side of him, joining their hands in his.

The lights came up as the curtain reopened. The audience renewed its furious applause, and suddenly he understood. Feeling a flood of warmth and a special sense of gratitude, Dominic Kazan stepped forward to take his bow.

Playwright. Actor. Son.

The rehearsals were finally over.

Thomas Ligotti

THE MEDUSA

"The most startling and unexpected literary discovery since Clive Barker" is how The Washington Post *described the bizarre stories of Thomas Ligotti. He has worked for a number of years in the small presses, but recent professional appearances include* The Magazine of Fantasy & Science Fiction, Weird Tales, *and the anthologies* Prime Evil, Fine Frights, Best New Horror 1 and 2 *and* The Year's Best Fantasy and Horror. *Tom first appeared in* FT *back in 1982 when we published 'The Frolic', while his story 'The Spectacles in the Drawer' was featured in our previous issue. Robinson/Carroll & Graf have recently published his second collection,* Grimscribe: His Lives and Works, *relating the adventures of the scientist of the title in the shadow world of the paranormal.*

I

Before leaving his room for the first time in nobody knows how long, Lucian Dregler transcribed a few stray thoughts into his notebook.

The sinister, the terrible never deceive: the state in which they leave us is always one of enlightenment. And only this condition of vicious insight enables us a full grasp of the world, *all* things considered, just as a frigid melancholy grants us full possession of ourselves.

We may hide from horror only in the heart of horror.

Could I be so unique among dreamers, having courted the Medusa—my first and oldest companion—to the exclusion of all others? Would I have her respond to this sweet talk?

Relieved to have these fragments safely on the page rather than in some precarious mental notebook, where they were likely to become smudged or completely effaced, Dregler slipped into a relatively old overcoat, locked the door of his room behind him, and exited down innumerable staircases at the back of his apartment building. A winding series of seldomly travelled streets was his established route to a certain place he now and then frequented, though for time's sake—in order to *waste* it, that is—he chose even more uncommon and chaotic avenues. He was meeting an acquaintance he had not seen in quite a while.

The place was very dark, though no more than in past memory, and much more populated than it first appeared to Dregler's eyes. He paused at the doorway, slowly but unsystematically removing his gloves, while his vision, still exceptional, worked with the faint halos of illumination offered by lamps of tarnished metal, which were spaced so widely along the walls that the light of one lamp seemed barely to link up and propagate that of its neighbour. Gradually, then, the darkness sifted away, revealing the shapes beneath it: a beaming forehead with the glitter of wire-rimmed eyeglasses below, cigarette-holding and beringed fingers lying asleep on a table, shoes of shining leather which ticked lightly against Dregler's own as he now passed cautiously through the room. At the back stood a column of stairs coiling up to another level, which was more an appended platform, a little brow of balcony or a puny pulpit, than what one might call a sub-section of the establishment proper. This level was caged in at its brink with a railing constructed of the same rather wiry

74

Deep in the mirror opened another pair of eyes the color of wine-mixed water. (Art: Dreyfus)

and fragile material as the stairway, giving this area the appearance of a makeshift scaffolding. Rather slowly, Dregler ascended the stairs.

"Good evening, Joseph," Dregler said to the man seated at the table beside an unusually tall and narrow window. Joseph Gleer stared for a moment at the old gloves Dregler had tossed onto the table.

"You still have those same old gloves," he replied to the greeting, then lifted his gaze, grinning: "And that overcoat!"

Gleer stood up and the two men shook hands. Then they both sat down and Gleer, indicating the empty glass between them on the table, asked Dregler if he still drank brandy. Dregler nodded, and Gleer said "Coming up" before leaning over the rail a little ways and holding out two fingers in view of someone in the shadows below.

"Is this just a sentimental symposium, Joseph?" inquired the now uncoated Dregler.

"In part. Wait until we've got our drinks, so you can properly congratulate me." Dregler nodded again, scanning Gleer's face without any observable upsurge in curiosity. A former colleague from Dregler's teaching days, Gleer had always possessed an open zest for minor intrigues, academic or otherwise, and an addiction to the details of ritual and protocol, anything preformulated and with precedent. He also had a liking for petty secrets, as long as he was among those privy to them. For instance, in discussions—no matter if the subject was philosophy or old films—Gleer took an obvious delight in revealing, usually at some advanced stage of the dispute, that he had quite knowingly supported some treacherously absurd school of thought. His perversity confessed, he would then assist, and even surpass, his opponent in demolishing what was left of his old position, supposedly for the greater glory of disinterested intellects everywhere. But at the same time, Dregler saw perfectly well what Gleer was up to. And though it was not always easy to play into Gleer's hands, it was this secret counter-knowledge that provided Dregler's sole amusement in these mental contests, for

> Nothing that asks for your arguments is worth arguing, just as nothing that solicits your belief is worth believing. The real and the unreal lovingly cohabit *in our terror*, the only "sphere" that matters.

Perhaps secretiveness, then, was the basis of the two men's relationship, a flawed secretiveness in Gleer's case, a consummate one in Dregler's.

Now here he was, Gleer, keeping Dregler in so-called suspense. His eyes, Dregler's, were aimed at the tall narrow window, beyond which were the bare upper branches of an elm that twisted with spectral movements under one of the floodlights fixed high upon the outside walls. But every few moments Dregler glanced at Gleer, whose babylike features were so remarkably unchanged: the cupid's bow lips, the cookie-dough cheeks, the tiny grey eyes now almost buried within the flesh of a face too often screwed up with laughter.

A woman with two glasses on a cork-bottomed tray was standing over the table. While Gleer paid for the drinks, Dregler lifted his and held it in the position of a lazy salute. The woman who had brought the drinks looked briefly and without expression at toastmaster Dregler. Then she went away and Dregler, with false ignorance, said: "To your upcoming or recently passed event, whatever it may be or have been."

"I hope it will be for life this time, thank you, Lucian."

"What is this, *quintus*?"

"*Quartus*, if you don't mind."

"Of course, my memory is as bad as my powers of observation. Actually I was looking for something shining on your finger, when I should have seen the shine of your eyes. No ring, though, from the bride?"

Gleer reached into his open shirt and pulled out a length of neck-chain, dangling at the end of which was a tiny rose-coloured diamond in a plain silver setting.

"Modern innovations," he said neutrally, replacing the chain and stone. "The moderns must have them, I suppose, but marriage is still marriage."

"Here's to the Middle Ages," Dregler said with unashamed weariness.

"And the middle-aged," refrained Gleer.

The men sat in silence for some moments. Dregler's eyes moved once more around that shadowy loft, where a few table shared the light of a single lamp. Most of its dim glow backfired onto the wall, revealing the concentric coils of the wood's knotty surface. Taking a calm sip of his drink, Dregler waited.

"Lucian," Gleer finally began in a voice so quiet that it was nearly inaudible.

"I'm listening," Dregler assured him.

"I didn't ask you here just to commemorate my marriage. It's been almost a year, you know. Not that that would make any difference to you."

Dregler said nothing, encouraging Gleer with receptive silence.

"Since that time," Gleer continued, "my wife and I have both taken leaves from the university and have been traveling, mostly in Europe and the Mediterranean. We've just returned a few days ago. Would you like another drink? You went through that one rather quickly."

"No, thank you. Please go on," Dregler requested very politely.

After drinking the last of his brandy, Gleer continued. "Lucian, I've never understood your fascination with what you call the Medusa. I'm not sure I care to, though I've never told you that. But through no deliberate efforts of my own, let me emphasize, I think I can further your, I guess you could say, pursuit. You are still interested in the matter, aren't you?"

"Yes, but I'm too poor to affort Peloponnesian jaunts like the one you and your wife have just returned from. Was that what you had in mind?"

"Not at all. You needn't even leave town, which is the strange part, the real beauty of it. It's very complicated how I know what I know. Wait a second. Here, take this."

Gleer now produced an object he had earlier stowed away somewhere in the darkness, laying it on the table. Dregler stared at the book. It was bound in a rust-coloured cloth and the gold lettering across its spine was flaking away. From what Dregler could make out of the remaining fragments of the letters, the title of the book seemed to be: *Electro-Dynamics for the Beginner*.

"What is this supposed to be?" he asked Gleer.

"Only a kind of passport, meaningless in itself. This is going to sound ridiculous—how I know it!—but you want to bring the book to this establishment," said Gleer, placing a business card upon the book's front cover, "and ask the owner how much he'll give you for it. I know you go to these shops all the time. Are you familiar with it?"

"Only vaguely," replied Dregler.

The establishment in question, as the business card read, was *Brother's Books: Dealers in Rare and Antiquarian Books, Libraries and Collections Purchased, Large Stock of Esoteric Sciences and Civil War, No Appointment Needed, Member of Manhattan Society of Philosophical Bookdealers, Benjamin Brothers, Founder and Owner*.

"I'm told that the proprietor of this place knows you by your writings," said Gleer, adding in an ambiguous monotone: "He thinks you're a real philosopher."

Dregler gazed at length at Gleer, his long fingers abstractedly fiddling with the little card. "Are you telling me that the Medusa is supposed to be a book?" he said.

Gleer stared down at the table-top and then looked up. "I'm not telling you anything I do not know for certain, which is not a great deal. As far as I know, it could still be anything you can imagine, and perhaps already have. Of course you can take this imperfect information however you like, as I'm sure you will. If you want to know more than I do, then pay a visit to this bookstore."

"Who told you to tell me this?" Dregler calmly asked.

"You can't ask that, Lucian. Everything falls apart if you do."

"Very well," said Dregler, pulling out his wallet and inserting the business card into it. He stood up and began putting on his coat. "Is that all, then? I don't mean to be rude but—"

"Why should you be any different from the usual? But one more thing I should tell you. Please sit down. Now listen to me. We've known each other a long time, Lucian. And I know how much this means to you. So whatever happens, or doesn't happen, I don't want you to hold me responsible. I've only done what I thought you yourself would want me to do. Well, tell me if I was right."

Dregler stood up again and tucked the book under his arm. "Yes, I suppose. But I'm sure we'll be seeing each other. Good night, Joseph."

"One more drink," offered Gleer.

"No, good night," answered Dregler.

As he started away from the table, Dregler, to his embarrassment, nearly rapped his head against a massive wooden beam which hung hazardously low in the darkness. He glanced back to see if Gleer had noticed this clumsy mishap. And after merely a single drink! But Gleer was looking the other way, gazing out the window at the tangled tendrils of the elm and the livid complexion cast upon it by the floodlights fixed high upon the outside wall.

For some time Dregler thoughtlessly observed the wind-blown trees outside before turning away to stretch out on his bed, which was a few steps from the window of his room. Beside him now was a copy of his first book, *Meditations on the Medusa*. He picked it up and read piecemeal from its pages.

> The worshipants of the Medusa, including those who clog pages with "insights" and interpretations such as these, are the most hideous citizens of this earth—and the most numerous. But

how many of them *know* themselves as such? Conceivably there may be an inner cult of the Medusa, but then again: who could dwell on the existence of such beings for the length of time necessary to round them up for execution?

It is possible that only the dead are not in league with the Medusa. We, on the other hand, are her allies—but always against ourselves. How does one become her *companion* . . . and live?

We are never in danger of beholding the Medusa. For that to happen she needs our consent. But a far greater disaster awaits those who know the Medusa to be gazing at them and long to reciprocate in kind. What better definition of a marked man: one who "has eyes" for the Medusa, whose eyes have a will and a fate of their own.

Ah, to be a thing without eyes. What a break to be *born* a stone!

Dregler closed the book and then replaced it on one of the shelves across the room. On that overcrowded shelf, leather and cloth pressing against cloth and leather, was a fat notebook stuffed with loose pages. Dregler brought this back to the bed with him and began rummaging through it. Over the years the folder had grown enormously, beginning as a few random memoranda—clippings, photographs, miscellaneous references which Dregler copied out by hand—and expanding into a storehouse of infernal serendipity, a testament of terrible coincidence. And the subject of every entry, major and minor, of this inadvertent encyclopedia was the Medusa herself.

Some of the documents fell into a section marked "Facetious," including a comic book (which Dregler picked off a drugstore rack) that featured the Medusa as a benevolent superheroine who used her hideous powers only on equally hideous foes in a world without beauty. Others belonged under the heading of "Irrelevant," where was placed a three-inch strip from a decades-old sports page lauding the winning season of "Mr. (*sic*) Medusa". There was also a meager division of the notebook which had no official designation, but which Dregler could not help regarding as items of "True Horror." Prominent among these was a feature article from a British scandal sheet: a photoless chronicle of a man's year-long suspicion that his wife was periodically possessed by the serpent-headed demon, a senseless little guignol which terminated with the wife's decapitation while she lay sleeping one night and the subsequent incarceration of a madman.

One of the least creditable subclasses of the notebook consisted of pseudo-data taken from the less legitimate propogators of mankind's knowledge: renegade "scientific" journals, occult-anthropology newsletters, and publications of various Centers of sundry "mythic" studies. Contributions to the notebook from periodicals such as *The Excentaur*, a back issue of which Dregler stumbled across in none other than Brother's Books, were collectively categorized as "Medusa and Medusans: Sightings and Material Explanations." An early number of this publication included an article which attributed the birth of the Medusa, and of all life on Earth, to one of many extraterrestrial visitors, for whom this planet has been a sort of truckstop or comfort station en route to other locales in other galactic systems.

All such enlightening finds Dregler relished with a surly joy, especially those proclamations from the high priests of the human mind and soul, who invariably relegated the Medusa to a psychic underworld where she serves as the image par excellence of romantic panic. But unique among the curiosities he cherished was an outburst of prose whose author seemed to follow in Dregler's own footsteps: a man *after his own heart*. "Can we be delivered," this writer rhetorically queried, "from the 'life force' as symbolized by Medusa? Can this energy, if such a thing exists, be put to death, crushed? Can we, in the arena of our being, come stomping out—gladiator-like—net and trident in hand, and, poking and swooping, pricking and swishing, *torment* this soulless and hideous demon into an excruciating madness, and, finally, annihilate it to the thumbs-down delight of our nerves and to our soul's deafening applause?" Unfortunately, however, these words were written in the meanest spirit of sarcasm by a critic who parodically reviewed Dregler's own *Meditations on the Medusa* when it first appeared twenty years earlier.

But Dregler never sought out reviews of his books, and the curious thing, the amazing thing, was that this item, like all the other bulletins and ponderings on the Medusa, had merely fallen into his hands unbidden. (In a dentist's office, of all places.) Though he had read widely in the lore of and commentary on the Medusa, none of the material in his rather haphazard notebook was attained through the normal channels of research. None of it was gained in an official manner, none of it foreseen. In the fewest words, it was all a gift of unforeseen circumstances, strictly unofficial matter.

But what did this prove, exactly, that he continued to be offered these pieces to his puzzle? It proved nothing, exactly or otherwise, and was merely a side-effect of his preoccupation with a single subject. Naturally he would be alert to its intermittent cameos on the stage of daily routine. This was normal. But although these "finds" proved nothing, rationally, they always did suggest more to Dregler's imagination than to his reason, especially when he pored over the collective contents of these archives devoted to his oldest companion.

It was, in fact, a reference to this kind of imagination for which he was now searching as he lay on his bed. And there it was, a paragraph he had once copied in the library from a little yellow book entitled *Things Near and Far*. "There is nothing in the nature of things," the quotation ran, "to prevent a man from seeing a dragon or a griffin, a gorgon or a unicorn. Nobody as a matter of fact has seen a woman whose hair consisted of snakes, nor a horse from whose forehead a horn projected; though very early man probably did see dragons—known to science as pterodactyls—and monsters more improbable than griffins. At any rate, none of these zoological fancies violates the fundamental laws of the intellect; the monsters of heraldry and mythology do not exist, but there is no reason in the nature of things nor in the laws of the mind why they should not exist."

It was therefore in line with the nature of things that Dregler suspended all judgements until he could pay a visit to a certain bookstore.

II

And it was late the following afternoon, emerging from daylong doubts and procrastinations, that Dregler entered a little slot-like shop squeezed between a grey building and a brown one. Nearly within arm's reach of each other, the opposing walls of the shop were solid with books. The higher shelves were all but unreachable except by means of a very tall ladder, and the highest shelves were apparently not intended for access. Back numbers of old magazines—*Blackwood's*, *The Spectator*, the *London* and *American Mercury's*—were stacked in plump, orderless piles by the front window, their pulpy covers dying in the sunlight. Missing pages from forgotten novels were stuck forever to a patch of floor or curled up in corners. Dregler noted page two hundred and two of *The Second Staircase* at his feet, and he couldn't help feeling a sardonic sympathy for the anonymous pair of eyes confronting an unexpected dead end in the narrative of that old mystery. Then again, he wondered, how many thousands of these volumes had already been browsed for the last time. This included, of course, the one he held in his own hand and for which he now succumbed to a brief and absurd sense of protectiveness. Dregler blamed his friend Gleer for this subtle aspect of what he suspected was a farce of far larger and cruder design.

Sitting behind a low counter in the telescopic distance of the rear of the store, a small and flabby man with wire-rimmed glasses was watching him. When Dregler approached the counter and lay the book upon it, the man—Benjamin Brothers—hopped alertly to his feet.

"Help you?" he asked. The bright tone of his voice was the formal and familiar greeting of an old servant.

Dregler nodded, vaguely recognizing the little man from a previous visit to his store some years ago. He adjusted the book on the counter, simply to draw attention to it, and said: "I don't suppose it was worth my trouble to bring this sort of thing here."

The man smiled politely. "You're correct in that, sir. Old texts like that, worth practically nothing to no one. Now down there in my basement," he said, gesturing toward a narrow doorway, "I've got literally thousands of things like that. Other things too, you know. The *Bookseller's Trade* called it 'Benny's Treasurehouse'. But maybe you're just interested in selling books today."

"Well, it seems that as long as I'm here . . ."

"Help yourself, Dr. Dregler," the man said warmly as Dregler started toward the stairway. Hearing his name, Dregler paused and nodded back at the bookdealer; then he proceeded down the stairs.

Dregler now recalled the basement of this store, along with the three lengthy flights of stairs needed to reach its unusual depths. The narrow street-level above was no more than a messy little closet in comparison to the expansive disorder down below: a cavern of clutter, all heaps and mounds, with bulging tiers of bookshelves laid out according to no easily observable scheme. It was a universe constructed solely of the softly jagged brickwork of books. But if the Medusa was a book, how would he ever find it in this chaos? And if it was not, what other definite form could he expect to encounter of a phenomenon which he had avoided precisely defining all these years, one whose most nearly exact emblem was a hideous woman with a head of serpents?

For some time he merely wandered around the crooked aisles and deep niches of the basement. Every so often he took down some book whose appearance caught his interest, unwedging it from an indistinct mass of battered spines and rescuing it before years rooted to the same spot caused its words to mingle with others among the ceaseless volumes of "Benny's Treasurehouse", fusing them all into a bonded babble of senseless, unseen pages. Opening the book, he leaned a threadbare shoulder against the towering, filthy stacks. And after spending very little time in the cloistered desolation of that basement, Dregler found himself yawning openly and scratching himself unconsciously, as if he were secluded in some personal sanctum.

But suddenly he became aware of this assumption of privacy which had instilled itself in him, and the feeling instantly perished, perhaps because he suspected its deception. Now his sense of a secure isolation was replaced, at all levels of creaturely response, by its opposite. For hadn't he written that "personal well-being serves solely to excavate within your soul a chasm which waits to be filled by a landslide of dread, an empty mould whose peculiar dimensions will one day manufacture the shapes of your *unique* terror."

Whether or not it was the case, Dregler felt that he was no longer, or perhaps never had been, alone in the chaotic treasurehouse. But he continued acting as if he were, omitting only the yawns and the scratchings. Long ago he had discovered that a mild flush of panic was a condition capable, in certain strange and unknown ways, of *seasoning* one's more tedious moments. So he did not immediately attempt to discourage this probably delusory sensation. However, like any state dependent upon the play of delicate and unfathomable forces, Dregler's mood or intuition was subject to unexpected metamorphoses.

And when Dregler's mood or intuition passed into a new phase, his surroundings followed close behind: both he and the treasurehouse simultaneously crossed the boundary which divides playful panics from those of a more lethal nature. But this is not to say that one kind of apprehension was more excusable than the other; they were equally opposed to the likings of logic. ("Regarding dread, intensity in itself is no assurance of validity.") So it meant nothing, necessarily, that the twisting aisles of books appeared to be tightening around the suspicious bibliophile, that the shelves now looked more conspicuously over-swollen with their soft and musty stock, that faint shufflings and shadows seemed to be frolicking like a fugue through the dust and dimness of the underground treasurehouse. Could he, as he turned the next corner, be led to see that which should not be seen?

The next corner, as it happened, was the kind one enters rather than turns—a cul-de-sac of bookshelves forming three walls which nearly reached the rafters of the ceiling. Dregler found himself facing the rear wall like a bad schoolboy in punishment. He gazed up and down its height as if contemplating whether or not it was real, pondering if one could simply pass through it once one had conquered the illusion of its solidity. Just as he was about to turn and abandon this nook, something lightly brushed against his left shoulder. With involuntary suddenness he pivoted in this direction, only to feel the same airy caress now squarely across his back. Continuing counterclockwise, he executed one full revolution until he was standing and staring at someone who was standing and staring, back at him from the exact spot where he, a mere moment before, had been standing.

The woman's high-heeled boots put her face at the same level as his, while her turban-like hat made her appear somewhat taller. It was fastened on the right side, Dregler's left, with a metal clasp studded with watery pink stones. From beneath her hat a few strands of straw-coloured hair sprouted onto a triangle of unwrinkled forehead. Then a pair of tinted eyeglasses, then a pair of unlipsticked lips, and finally a high-collared coat which descended as a dark, elegant cylinder down to her boots. She calmly withdrew a pad of paper from one of her pockets, tore off the top page, and presented it to Dregler.

"Sorry if I startled you," it said.

After reading the note, Dregler looked up at the woman and saw that she was gently chopping her hand against her neck, but only a few times and merely to indicate some vocal disability. Laryngitis? wondered Dregler, or something chronic. He examined the note once again and observed the name, address, and telephone number of a company that serviced furnaces and air-conditioners. This, of course, told him nothing.

The woman then tore off a second pre-written message from the pad and pressed it into Dregler's already paper-filled palm, smiling at him very deliberately as she did so. (How he wanted to see what her eyes were doing!) She shook his hand a little before taking away hers and making a silent, scentless exit. So what was that reek Dregler detected in the air when he stared down at the note, which simply read: "Regarding M."

And below this word-and-a-half message was an address, and below that was a specified time on the following day. The handwriting was nicely formed, the most attractive Dregler had ever seen.

In light of the past few days, Dregler almost expected to find still another note waiting for him when he returned home. It was folded in half and stuffed underneath the door to his apartment. "Dear Lucian," it began, "just when you think things have reached their limit of ridiculousness, they become more ridiculous still. In brief—we've been had! Both of us. And by my wife, no less, along with a friend of hers. (A blond-haired anthropology prof whom I think you may know, or know of; at any rate she knows you, or at least your writings, maybe both.) I'll explain the whole thing when we meet, which I'm afraid won't be until my wife and I get back from another jaunt. (Eyeing some more islands, this time in the Pacific.)

"I was hoping that you would be skeptical enough not to go to the bookstore, but after finding you not at home I feared the worst. Hope you didn't have your hopes up, which I don't think has ever happened to you anyway. No harm done, in any case. The girls explained to me that it was a quasi-scientific hoax they were perpetrating, a recondite practical joke. If you think you were taken in, you can't imagine how I was. You can't believe how real and serious they made the whole ruse seem to me.

But if you got as far as the bookstore, you know by now that the punch line to the joke was a pretty weak one. The whole point, as I was told, was merely to stir your interest just enough to get you to perform some mildly ridiculous act. I'm curious to know how Mr. B. Bros. reacted when the distinguished author of *Meditations on the Medusa* and other ruminative volumes presented him with a hopelessly worthless old textbook.

"Seriously, I hope it caused you no embarrassment, and both of us, all *three* of us, apologize for wasting your time. See you soon, tanned and pacified by a South Sea Eden. And we have plans for making the whole thing up to you, that's a promise."

The note was signed, of course, by Joseph Gleer.

But Gleer's confession, though it was evident to Dregler that he himself believed it, was no more convincing than his "lead" on a Bookstore Medusa. Because this lead, which Dregler had not credited for a moment, led further than Gleer, who no longer credited it, had knowledge of. So it seemed that while his friend had now been placated by a false illumination, Dregler was left to suffer alone the effects of a true state of unknowing. And whoever was behind this hoax, be it a true one or a false, knew the minds of both men very well.

Dregler took all the notes he had received that day, paper-clipped them together, and put them into a new section of his massive scrapbook. He tentatively labelled this section: "Personal Confrontations with the Medusa, Either Real or Apparent."

III

The address given to Dregler the day before was not too far for him to walk, restive peripatetic that he was. But for some reason he felt rather fatigued that morning; so he hired a taxi to speed him across a drizzle-darkened city. Settling into the spacious dilapidation of the taxi's back seat, he took note of a few things. Why, he wondered, were the driver's glasses, which every so often filled the rear-view mirror, even darker than the day? Did she make a practice of thus "admiring" all her passengers? And was this back-seat debris—the "L"-shaped cigarette butt on the door's armrest, the black apple core on the floor—supposed to serve as objects of *their* admiration? Dregler questioned a dozen other things about this routine ride, this drenched day, and the city outside where umbrellas multiplied like mushrooms in the greyness; and he was now satisfied with his lack of a sense of well-being. Earlier he was concerned that his flow of responses that day would not be those of a man who was possibly about to confront the Medusa. He was apprehensive that he might look on this ride and its destination with lively excitement or as an adventure of some kind; in brief, he feared that his attitude would prove, to a certain extent, to be one of insanity. To be sane, he held, was either to be sedated by melancholy or activated by hysteria, two responses which are "always and equally warranted for those of *sound* insight." All others were irrational, merely symptoms of imaginations left idle, of memories out of work. And above these mundane responses, the only elevation allowable, the only valid transcendence, was a sardonic one: a bliss that annihilated the visible universe with jeers of dark joy, a *mindful* ecstasy. Anything else in the way of "mysticism" was a sign of deviation or distraction, and a heresy to the obvious.

The taxi turned onto a block of wetted brownstones, stopping before a tiny streetside lawn overhung by the skeletal branches of two baby birch trees. Dregler paid the driver, who expressed no gratitude whatever for the tip, and walked quickly through the drizzle toward a golden-bricked building with black numbers—two-o-two—above a black door with a brass knob and knocker. Reviewing the information on the crumpled piece of paper he took from his pocket, Dregler pressed the glowing bell-button. There was no one else in sight along the street, its trees and pavement fragrantly damp.

The door opened and Dregler stepped swiftly inside. A shabbily dressed man of indefinite age closed the door behind

him, then asked in a cordially nondescript voice: "Dregler?"
He nodded in reply. After a few reactionless moments the man
moved past Dregler, waving once for him to follow down the
ground-floor hallway. They stopped at a door that was directly
beneath the main stairway leading to the upper floors. "In
here," said the man, placing his hand upon the doorknob.
Dregler noticed the ring, its rosewater stone and silver
band, and the disjunction between the man's otherwise dour
appearance and this comparatively striking piece of jewelry.
The man pushed open the door and, without entering the
room, flipped a light-switch on the inside wall.

To all appearances it was an ordinary storeroom cluttered
with a variety of objects. "Make yourself comfortable," the man
said as he indicated to Dregler the way into the room. "Leave
whenever you like, just close the door behind you."

Dregler gave a quick look around the room. "Isn't there
anything else," he asked meekly, as if he were the stupidest
student of the class. "This is it, then?" he persisted in a quieter,
more dignified voice.

"This is it," the man echoed softly. Then he slowly closed the
door, and from inside Dregler could hear the footsteps walking
back down the hallway and up the staircase above the room.

The room was an average understairs niche, and its ceiling
tapered downward into a smooth slant where angular steps
ascended upward on the other side. Elsewhere its outline
was obscure, confused by huge bedsheets shaped like lamps
or tables or small horses; heaps of rocking chairs and baby-
chairs and other items of broken furniture; bandaged hoses
that drooped like dead pythons from hooks on the walls; animal
cages whose doors hung open on a single hinge; old paint cans
and pale tarps speckled like an egg; and a dusty light fixture
that cast a grey haze over everything.

Somehow there was not a variety of smells imperfectly
mingled in the room, each telling the tale of its origin, but only
a single smell pieced like a puzzle out of many: its complete
image was dark as the shadows in a cave and writhing in a

dozen directions over curving walls. Dregler gazed around the room, picked up some small object and immediately set it down again because his hands were trembling. He found himself a solid carton of something to sit on, kept his eyes open, and waited.

Afterward he couldn't remember how long he had stayed in the room, though he did manage to store up every nuance of the eventless vigil for later use in his voluntary and involuntary dreams. (They were compiled into that increasingly useful section marked "Personal Confrontations with the Medusa", a section that was fleshing itself out as a zone swirling with red shapes and a hundred hissing voices.) Dregler recalled vividly, however, that he left the room in a state of panic after catching a glimpse of himself in an old mirror that had a hair-line fracture slithering up its center. On his way out he lost his breath when he felt himself being pulled back into the room. But it was only a loose thread from his overcoat that had gotten caught in the door. It finally snapped cleanly off and he was free to go, his heart livened with dread.

And he never let on to his friends what a success that afternoon had been for him, not that he could have explained it to them in any practical way even if he desired to. As promised, they did make up for any inconvenience or embarrassment Dregler might have suffered as a result of, in Gleer's words, the "bookstore incident". The three of them held a party in Dregler's honor, and he finally met Gleer's new wife and her accomplice in the "hoax". (It became apparent to Dregler that no one, least of all himself, would admit it had gone further than that.) Dregler was left alone with this woman for only a brief time, and in the corner of a crowded room. While each of them knew of the other's work, this seemed to be the first time they had personally met. Nonetheless, they both confessed to a feeling of their prior acquaintance without being able, or willing, to substantiate its origins. And although plenty of mutually known parties were established, they failed to find any direct link between the two of them.

"Maybe you were a student of mine," Dregler suggested.

She smiled and said: "Thank you, Lucian, but I'm not as young as you seem to think."

Then she was jostled from behind ("Whoops," said a tipsy academic), and something she had been fiddling with in her hand ended up in Dregler's drink. It turned the clear bubbling beverage into a glassful of liquid rose-light.

"I'm so sorry. Let me get you another," she said, and then disappeared into the crowd.

Dregler fished the earring out of the glass and stole away with it before she had a chance to return with a fresh drink. Later in his room he placed it in a small box, which he labelled: "Treasures of the Medusa."

But there was nothing he could prove and he knew it.

IV

It was not many years later that Dregler was out on one of his now famous walks around the city. Since the bookstore incident, he had added several new titles to his works, and these had somehow gained him the faithful and fascinated audience of readers that had previously eluded him. Prior to his "discovery" he had been accorded only a distant interest in critical and popular circles alike, but now every little habit of his, not the least of all his daily meanderings, had been turned by commentators into "typifying traits" and "defining quirks". "Dregler's walks," stated one article, "are a constitutional of the modern mind, urban journeys by a tortured Ulysses *sans* Ithaca." Another article offered this back-cover superlative: "the most baroque inheritor of Existentialism's obsessions."

But whatever fatuosities they may have inspired, his recent books—*A Bouquet of Worms, Banquet for Spiders,* and *New Meditations on the Medusa*—had enabled him to "grip the minds of a dying generation and pass on to them his pain".

These words were written, rather uncharacteristically, by Joseph Gleer in a highly favorable review of *New Meditations* for a philosophical quarterly. He probably thought they might revive his friendship with his old colleague, but Dregler never acknowledged Gleer's effort, nor the repeated invitations to join his wife and him for some get-together or other. What else could Dregler do? Whether Gleer knew it or not, he was now one of them. And so was Dregler, though his saving virtue was an awareness of this disturbing fact. And this was part of his pain.

"We can only live by leaving our 'soul' in the hands of the Medusa," Dregler wrote in *New Meditations*. "Whether she is an angel or a gargoyle is not the point. Each merely allows us a gruesome diversion from some ultimate catastrophe which would turn us to stone; each is a mask hiding the *worst* visage, a medicine that numbs the mind. And the Medusa will see to it that we are protected, sealing our eyelids closed with the gluely spittle of her snakes, while their bodies elongate and slither past our lips to devour us *from the inside*. This is what we must never witness, except in the imagination, where it is a charming sight. And in the word, no less than in the mind, the Medusa fascinates much more than she appalls, and haunts us just *this side* of petrification. On the other side is the unthinkable, the unheard-of, that-which-should-not-be: hence, the Real. This is what throttles our souls with a hundred fingers—somewhere, perhaps in that dim room which caused us to forget ourselves, that place where we left ourselves behind amid shadows and strange sounds—while our minds and words toy, like playful, stupid pets, with *diversions* of an immeasurable disaster. The tragedy is that we must steer so close in order to avoid this hazard. *We may hide from horror only in the heart of horror.*"

Now Dregler had reached the outermost point of his daily walk, the point at which he usually turned and made his way back to his apartment, that *other* room. He gazed at the black door with the brass knob and knocker, glancing away to the street's porchlights and lofty bay windows which were glowing like mad in the late dusk. From bluish streetlights hung downward domes: inverted halos or open eyes. Then, for the first time in the history of these excursions, a light rain began to sprinkle down, nothing very troublesome. But in the next moment Dregler had already sought shelter in the welcoming brownstone.

He soon came to stand before the door of the room, keeping his hands deep in the pockets of his overcoat and away from temptation. Nothing had changed, he noticed, nothing at all. The door had not been opened by anyone since he had last closed it behind him on that hectic day years ago. And there was the proof, as he knew, somehow, it would be: that long thread from his coat still dangled from where it had been caught between door and frame. Now there was no question about what he would do.

It was to be a quick peek through a hand-wide crack, but enough to risk disillusionment and the dispersal of all the charming traumas he had articulated in his brain and books, scattering them like those peculiar shadows he supposed lingered in that room. And the voices, would he hear that hissing which heralded her presence as much as the flitting red shapes? He kept his eyes fixed upon his hand on the doorknob as it nudged open the door. So the first thing he saw was the way it, his hand, took on a rosy dawn-like glow, then a deeper twilight crimson as it was bathed more directly by the odd illumination within the room.

There was no need to reach in and flick the lightswitch just inside. He could see quite enough as his vision, still exceptional, was further aided by the way a certain cracked mirror was positioned, giving his eyes a reflected entrance into the dim depths of the room. And in the depths of the mirror? A split-image, something fractured by a thread-like chasm that oozed up a viscous red glow. There was a man in the mirror; no, not a man but a mannikin, or a frozen figure of some kind. It was naked and rigid, leaning against a wall of clutter, its arms outstretching and reaching behind, as if trying to break a backwards fall.

Its head was also thrown back, almost broken-necked; its eyes were pressed shut into a pair of well-sealed creases, two ocular wrinkles which had taken the place of the sockets themselves. And its mouth gaped so widely with a soundless scream that all wrinkles had been smoothed away from that part of the old face.

He barely recognized this face, this naked and paralyzed form which he had all but forgotten, except as a lurid figure of speech he once used to describe the uncanny condition of his soul. But it was no longer a charming image of the imagination. Reflection had given it charm, made it acceptable to sanity, just as reflection had made those snakes, and the one who wore them, picturesque and not petrifying. But no amount of reflection could have conceived seeing the thing itself, nor the state of being stone.

The serpents were moving now, coiling themselves about the ankles and wrists, the neck; stealthily entering the screaming man's mouth and prying at his eyes. Deep in the mirror opened another pair of eyes the color of wine-mixed water, and through a dark tangled mass they glared. The eyes met his, but not in a mirror. And the mouth was screaming, but made no sound. Finally, he was reunited, in the worst possible way, with the thing within the room.

Stiff inside of stone now, he heard himself think. *Where is the world, my words?* No longer any world, any words, there would only be that narrow room and himself and the oldest companion of his soul. Nothing other than that would exist for him, could exist, nor, in fact, had ever existed. In its own rose-tinted heart, his horror had at last found him.

Edward Darton

REJUVENATION

Goliath ebon skulls protrude from writhing copper sand
seared, I weep neath fiery funneling clouds
meshed with molten fury
as I race over jetbone splinters by a leaden boiling sea
past spindly husks like dead leaves lain
pierced by black skeletal fingers
I woke with dampened linen
clutched in trembling hands
and felt beneath me on the sheets
grains of crawling sand

Tonight I ran once more across the alien shore of the dead
and stumbling fell impaled upon a charnel demon's claw
my scarlet fountain drunk greedily
by the animate thirsting sand
the skulls, now sheathed in spongy green flesh
struggled up from the strand
the ghastly shore was heaved
in the midst of a mighty quake
I swam into a black void
nevermore to wake

Kathryn Ptacek

LIVING TO THE END

Kathryn A. Ptacek was raised in Albuquerque, New Mexico, where she received her B.A. in journalism from the University of New Mexico. She currently lives in New Jersey and is married to horror writer Charles L. Grant. Since the mid-1970s she has written many novels, including a historical fantasy series, five horror novels, and historical romances under several pseud-onyms. Her latest genre titles are Ghost Dance *and* In Silence Sealed, *both from Tor Books. Dark fantasy short stories have been published in* Greystone Bay, Doom City, Post Mortem, Pulphouse, Eldritch Tales, The Horror Show *and others, and she has been awarded both the Silver and Gold Medal awards for genre fiction by the* West Coast Review of Books. *Kathryn is also the editor of three anthologies,* Women of Darkness I *and* II *(Tor Books) and* Women of the West *(Doubleday). She makes her de-but in* Fantasy Tales *with the following dark and morbid chiller.*

"**H**e really is a mean old man," a youthful voice whispered fiercely from somewhere in the greyness. "He deserves to die."

"Emily!" A flutter of material, an old-fashioned handkerchief, perhaps. The scent of roses, flowers on the table.

"It's true, Mom," the girl said. "He never did anything good in his life. You know that. He never says anything nice about anyone—just last week he called you a bitch—after all you've done for him."

"Don't say that word, please."

"But he called you that—I heard him, the neighbours probably hear him. And that's not right. He should be more appreciative of you. You've done so much for him."

"I'm not looking for any one to thank me. I did what I had to do, Em. I've told you that before."

"I know. But it's still not right. Not at all." An impatient movement, a hand slamming down on a jean-clad thigh then.

"Well, no, dear, it's not. I'm sure he didn't really mean what he said. After all, you know how it is when they get older. They don't remember things as clearly as they once did, they aren't as patient as they used to be; things seem so different—"

"Mom."

"Well, they do!"

"I know, but it doesn't excuse the hell he's given you these past five years."

Silence from the older woman.

Then the girl: "We'll all be glad when he dies. You, me, everyone. I hope it's soon!"

"Emily, you're talking about your grandfather!"

"I don't care. I don't! He doesn't love me, or you, or Grandma. None of us. And he never has."

"Hush, child, he might hear."

"I hope he does."

Weariness in the woman's voice. "Leave, Em, please, for a while, honey. You're just making things worse than they already are."

"All right, Mom. I'm sorry I upset you. But it's the truth."

There was the sound of a door closing, distant, aloof, and then through the greyness—

Remembered:

He had cheated death. He had escaped. (Art: David Benham).

The incredible surprise that this was even happening, then falling out of the immense tree, feeling the branches scratching him as he fell through them, stinging his skin and ripping his work clothes as he plummeted, the soil and earth rushing at him, smashing onto the ground, smashing, and smashing, and the explosion of white hot pain.

Oh yes, he remembered the pain. He remembered that when he recalled nothing else. There was nothing but the aching and throbbing inside him and outside him for days and weeks now. The pain so agonizing that it drove everything from his mind and memory.

Casts entombed his legs and arms, while something solid held his body firm, motionless. He was as helpless as an infant, dependent upon strangers, strangers who loomed at him out of the greyness.

He blinked in and out of consciousness occasionally to see the pallid faces of those people he knew had come to see him one last time, and they talked to him in those falsely cheerful tones he loathed, and spoke of everything they and their busy family were doing—why, it was a wonder they'd managed to even squeeze in this hospital visit—and of the weather, which he couldn't care less about, and the sports season, which he'd never liked anyway, but never once did they mention his accident.

Later he listened to his visitors outside in the hallway when they thought he couldn't possibly hear, and they said that he had been a foolish old man, that he should never have been pruning the tree up there, not at his age anyway, and there had been sobbing and the sound of a soothing voice.

And the old man knew. He was dying. He would never go home again; he would never leave the alienness of this damned hospital. Not now. He would stay there in the antiseptic whiteness, living to the end. He would breath and eat and . . . live?

Could this be called living, he wondered, when each one of his bodily functions was monitored by a quietly humming machine, whose red and amber eyes peered out of the curtained gloom of the hospital room at him? At his elbow loomed something vaguely shaped like a metal tree—the tree from which he'd fallen, he thought for a moment, then realized that was a delusion—and from its cold metallic branches hung four bottles trickling liquid into his collapsing veins.

Fruit for the dying, he thought wryly. Fruit of the glucose and antibiotics and painkillers and whatever else these modern doctors thought they should pump into his tired old system in their grandiose effort to keep him alive one more hour, one more day.

"Heroic efforts" these healers called it, unaware of the irony.

He saw his bruised wrist, grotesquely over-swollen from the seeping of intravenous liquids, where the tubes pierced his skin. He had been grafted, had become one with the tree now.

And there was a cold tube that thrust up into his nose, that wormed its way down into his old lungs, pumping out the fluid, dark and yellow, that filled them and obscured his breathing. And a tube had been inserted into his groin, the waste fluids flowing into a plastic bag hanging at the side of the bed. He couldn't even have the privacy of that any longer.

His throat hurt. He couldn't touch it, because he couldn't move, but he suspected he had had a tracheotomy to allow another tube to be shoved into his body. He saw an obscenely thick blue plastic hose snake away to a machine in which what looked like a small inverted accordion rose and fell. That kept him breathing.

Another heroic effort.

He coughed, a wracking liquid sound, and watched the needles on the monitor jump, the accordion pump up and down. He pulled his dry lips back into a smile.

He had pneumonia. He knew that now.

Elderly people usually got pneumonia when they went to the hospital. But then the doctors and nurses would cure it with their wonder drugs—usually—and the elderly people would get well eventually, and they would go home, more feeble than before, and they would live their lives until they got something else, something that hurt more, something more fatal than pneumonia.

In the old days, when he had been young, if he'd fallen from that tree and hurt himself this way, his family would have simply moved him into the front bedroom, and the family physician would have visited, and shaking his head sadly, would have pronounced his impending death. And there would have been no visit to the hospital, no effort to prolong, because nothing would have helped, nothing could be done. And maybe that was the way it should have been. Within a few hours, maybe days, he would have died, dignity intact, a whole man, not whittled away until he was something less human, something slightly more than a machine.

His uncle had been injured on the farm, had fallen into a piece of the machinery, and when the hired hands had found him, hours later, the man, only in his forties, had still clung somehow to life. They'd carried him back to the house, and the old man remembered visiting that very day. To say good-bye to his uncle, who was conscious to the very end. The man had been surrounded by those he loved and those who loved him, amid his own house, on his own farm. And he had died. Whole. With dignity.

His uncle had given him his watch, one of those old gold pocket types that hung from chains no one wore any more, and the old man had always cherished it, for it was the one thing that he had of his uncle, the one thing that would always recall the man's cheerful face and good-natured laugh and wonderful long-winded stories about the land and the animals. He'd had that watch in his pocket the day he fell out of the tree. When he landed, he had heard it crunch underneath him, and he knew then that after all this time it had finally been broken, and that had saddened him even more than his accident.

His accident.

The old man couldn't blame his wife or his daughter or even his granddaughter. Not really. They had just thought they were helping him when they called the ambulance and the emergency squad had picked up the bloody pieces and rushed him to this hell. They didn't know the agony he would be in. He didn't blame them. Not much.

He wished he could cry, but he was unable.

He had never thought he would die. Not really. Not consciously. He had always been so strong, so fit. Never been ill, not really, except for that one time in the sixties when he'd come down with that damned Hong Kong flu or whatever was going around then and had been laid up for nearly two weeks. Had never been to the hospital; he even had his appendix and tonsils yet. Not many old-timers could claim that, he thought proudly. He'd watched the others around him die, first his mother, then his father, aunts and uncles and cousins, his older brother and sisters. All gone before him. He lived on and on, and he knew that there was nothing to stop him.

Until now.

He heard a cheerful feminine voice, a youthful voice that had never suffered excruciating pain, and he knew it was time for some damned procedure that the hospitals insisted upon inflicting on sick people, like taking his temperature or his blood pressure or his pulse. And what did it matter any more, these silly things, he wondered, when he was going to die.

She left, and it was quiet again, except for the machines, the harshness of his breathing.

He hated the cards that the nurses read to him in their syrupy every-so-bright voices. "Get Well Soon" and "Hope You're On Your Feet Soon" and "Heard You Had An Accident!" some of them said. He would have laughed at those feeble sentiments, had he been able to. In his life he had sent many of those cards; how meaningless they had been, since all he'd done was scrawl his name under some patently syrupy sentiment. Far better if he'd sat down and written a personal note. But he hadn't. And now in a long life of few regrets, he regretted that.

He hated the phone calls—didn't everyone know they brought bad news? Phone calls which he received daily, even though his family and friends had been informed he couldn't talk. He heard his wife speaking in a low tone, and he hated it because he couldn't understand what she was saying, yet he knew it wasn't good.

But most of all, he hated the flowers. Especially the roses, because they reminded him of his mother. And he had not thought about her for a long time. He couldn't recall her face as well as he once had; it was more a shadowy form than anything solid. He couldn't remember her voice, either, except that it had been soft. After all, he had been only a small child when she died. But he did remember standing by her bedside and looking down at her wasted form and smelling the roses, their reeking perfume churning his empty stomach.

It was soon after that his father began spiraling downward into his own grave with the help of the bottle. And it was after his mother's death that his father began to beat him, and his older brother. And it was only a year later that his father had struck his brother too hard, once too often, and even though they rushed him to the hospital right away, the boy never came out of the coma. Dead at the age of thirteen. Dead by his own father's hand.

The drinking worsened, and every night his father came home from work and drank and shouted and cursed. He and his sisters kept to themselves. He did for himself; he would not ask his father for anything—not now. His younger brother retreated into a dream world, where no one could reach him, unless he allowed it.

He left home, then, at seventeen. His sisters and brother cried, but he couldn't stand it any longer. He had to be on his own. And that was the way it had been all his life, even after he married, even after he had children. Up to the end.

And now he was dependent upon someone else, upon something else for life, and he hated it. How he wished he could pull these hated tubes out of his body and fling them as far away as possible, but he couldn't. He could only lie there, and blink and think, and pass the time until his death.

And the days passed in a daze, a blur brought on by his medication and the extent of his injuries and all-consuming pain. He could mark the passage of time by the dripping of the fluids into his veins, by the smell of the dying flowers, by the malfunctioning of his body. Sometimes he saw his uncle in the room, and they would talk, sometimes the shadowy form of his mother, who would weep, and sometimes the old man would see his father. But for him the old man had no words.

The greyness seeped into him, even as the life-sustaining liquids did, and he dreamed, and woke, and didn't know the difference.

And now his family were all coming to bid him a farewell. They didn't say that, of course, but he knew. He wasn't dumb. He wasn't senile. He wasn't dead.

Yet.

There was his wife, and she was being absurdly brave, although her eyes were reddened; he could see that; and she sniffed a lot into her handkerchief. He wished he could hold her one last time, say that he was sorry for all the times he had yelled when he hadn't wanted to. But he couldn't. And his daughter, that pitiful bitch was there—she married a man weaker than herself—and her sassy brat. The girl's face was grim; he knew she wouldn't miss him. He grimaced at her, but because his teeth weren't in, it weakened the expression. She turned away. No doubt disgusted with him. And yet she was the most like him, of all the family. She would have hated to hear that, he thought. She would have denied it vehemently, but it was true, nonetheless. But what did she know yet? She was only fifteen; time enough for her to learn.

His younger brother, reeking of alcohol and who'd never said much in his entire life, but now who just clasped his hand tightly, while his sister-in-law, with her damned forties hair-do and heavily mascaraed eyes and prissy lips, couldn't meet his eyes. She kept blowing her nose. The hypocrite. He'd never liked her; she's always detested him for his independence, his non-need of the family. At least his good-for-nothing son wasn't there; had the good sense to stay away. The boy—no, the man—was too much like his grandfather.

They were a reassuring lot, the old man thought. No one spoke to him, no one reassured him that he would make it, after all; he supposed they had nothing left to say to him.

Well, he certainly didn't have anything left to say to them.

He endured. Day after day, long night after long night. One hospital shift after another, one cheerful nurse after one cheerful orderly. He saw the passing of light and dark through the oblong window across the room, and sometimes he thought he saw it raining. Days were passing. His life was passing. Trickling away with the seconds and minutes.

In and out of the greyness, voices like the humming of overhead wires.

He didn't know what he wanted. He wanted to live, he thought; he didn't want to die. But if he had to live like this, only half a man, if he couldn't be himself and get up and around—

If only he had another chance. Even with that, he wasn't sure.

And all he heard was the rasping of his breath, the thrumming of the machines, the harshness of the accordion. Up and down, *pause*, up and down, and up and—over and over until he hated the sound.

And the day had come, and the light in the room had flickered briefly then dimmed, and his wife's face had been floating above his own as she gazed with tears down at him, and he heard her first talking, almost pleading, then weeping, and beyond her in the greyness, he thought he saw someone else, a woman, but he couldn't be sure, couldn't see very well, and then:

He *escaped*.

When David Farrister woke up, he knew he was dead. He had died. Was gone. Passed over. Was no more.

Dust to dust.

And yet here he was in his all-too-familiar silver and maroon bedroom, in his own twenty-year-mortgaged home just a few miles north of Philadelphia, and not in the whiteness of a sterile hospital. Here he was surrounded comfortingly by the memorabilia and junk and incredible accumulation of all his thirty-seven years. Here he was.

Slightly dizzy, he got up, feeling the scratchiness of the faded carpet under his bare feet. One wadded sock stuck out from under the bed. He looked around the room, taking in the handmade bookcases along one wall, the numerous framed diplomas flanking the door, the nude drawing in charcoal that his mother had done once and which had shocked his grandmother. He grinned at the memory. The window was open and a brisk cool breeze caressed him and ghosted the sheer curtains back and forth. And he realized he was nude. Where were his pyjamas?

Frowning, he moved across the room, and jerked open the top drawer of the oak bureau. There they were. Tan with the blue trim, neatly folded up as he recalled. His fingers brushed the monogram. But he remembered putting them on last night. He had showered after Samantha left before midnight, and come in here, still dripping slightly, and pulled them out—

But here they were, fresh from the laundry, crisp and clean.

Frowning slightly, he scratched his side and stood there, looking down at his pyjamas, then at his toes, and remembered nothing at all.

Slowly David walked into the bathroom, flicked on the overhead light, and stared at himself in the full-length mirror.

The face there, with its taunt skin and wrinkle-less smoothness, and the day's growth of dark beard, that face there was of a young man. The body was that of a man in his prime. The eyes blue and bright, clear, unhazed with pain and death.

Why did he remember an old face: One with grizzled beard, and pouches, and sags, and seams? A body with broken bones? A hospital room filled with strangers who stared at him with sad eyes? A room filled with the scent of dying flowers?

Why?

109

Slowly, not understanding what had happened, he shaved, methodically, as if doing it for the first time. He splashed on his after-shave lotion, crisp and clean and *alive*, and rolled on his deodorant, smelling the almost medicinal freshness of it.

He dressed slowly, so slowly, so methodically. He selected each article of clothing carefully, and held his shoes as if he had never seen them before. They were expensive leather ones from Italy. He ran a finger along the gold-tipped toe. He frowned again. He was savouring, tasting all the activities he took for granted, all the day-to-day activities.

As if . . . as if . . . He grinned.

He knew what had happened.

He had cheated death. He had escaped. He had left one life—but entered another.

Smiling, he padded out into the sunny kitchen with its white laminate cabinets and Italian tile counters, and made a breakfast of dry cereal and cranberry juice and strong black tea, and as he sat in the tiny breakfast nook, he sipped and ate slowly, and stared out into the garden in the backyard, at the robins pulling up worms from his garden, at the starling nibbling at the tender young plants that struggled to live.

To live.

That's what he would do, again. He'd been given another chance.

Whistling, he picked up his leather briefcase from where he had tossed it on the couch the evening before—a lifetime ago, he told himself with a slight chuckle—and walked out the door of his house, past the rosebushes that were just beginning to bud. He glanced at them from the corner of his eye. He didn't like roses; he would have to have them dug up; would replace them with azaleas or something.

He walked down the street, and caught the bus into town and walked, taking long energetic strides, aware of the buildings for the first time, walked into his ad agency and nodded to his employees and talked to them and went to his office.

His secretary had a single white rose bud in a cut crystal vase on her desk. He smiled at her, and she smiled back.

"From an admirer?" he asked, nodding toward the rosebud.

Her overly plucked eyebrows drew together slightly. "Don't you recall?"

He smiled, forcing the expression. "Of course." He winked. She grinned.

He closed the door behind him and sat down behind the cluttered desk.

He began working.

And during the long hours of the morning none of the men or women in the agency noticed anything different. They treated him the same as always. But of course, he had seen them only the day before.

The day before. Before his death. He laughed softly to himself, then picked up his pen and began scribbling a note.

There was the usual amount of work, and new accounts to be reviewed, and an old client to take to lunch because she was thinking of leaving the agency after all this time but wasn't really sure she wanted to do that, and he needed to sweet-talk her into staying. The silly old bitch. He'd had a lot of trouble with her since he'd taken over, and he'd really preferred letting her go, but there was the money to consider. A hell of a lot of money.

And he did all this.

And at six-thirty he left the office—early finally, his secretary said with a smile—and napped as he took the bus back out to his street, and he was walking around the bus, and he was thinking ahead, thinking of the next day and all the appointments he knew he would have to keep even though he'd like to take some time off, when he heard the sound and realized something was *wrong*.

There was the squealing sound of brakes slammed on, the sound of something big skidding, and a long high-pitched shriek that seemed to be coming from his own throat—a throat that hurt because of the tubes, he could feel them, feel them snaking down his throat—and he saw the twin headlights bearing down on him, glowing red and amber, and then . . .

Darkness and the smell of roses.

When Mary Mike woke up out of the greyness, she knew she was dead. She had died. Was gone. Passed over. Was no more.
Dust to dust.
It had been a strange dream. She had dreamed she was a young man, a man in a strange city, who had—. She did not want to remember any more. She did not understand her dream, and it disturbed her greatly. She did not have many dreams.

She rose slowly, and still in her nightgown, said her prayers, facing the small silver crucifix on the white wall, and then crossed herself, and slowly, so slowly because the rheumatism was coming into her knees these days and she was always so stiff in the morning, she got to her feet and washed her face and her hands. She dressed and shuffled to breakfast.

She did not talk to the other sisters of her dream, for they were an order vowed to silence. During the meal, though, she watched the faces of the other women, almost twenty of them, and their faces were peaceful, serene, and very intent on the breakfast before them. Surely they did not have dreams such as hers.

She returned to her room for her missal and walked to the chapel, and there she talked to her confessor, just as she had done the day before, and the day before *that*, and each day she had been here.

And the priest said much the same thing he had that day before—that her sins were very small and thus only a tiny penance must be done, even though she knew he was wrong for her sins were great—and she knew that she must tell him of her strange dream, but she was afraid. Afraid that he would condemn her for dreaming of being in a man's body. Was this a sin? Mary Mike asked herself, confused. A sin to dream that? But, how much control did someone have over one's dreams?

In the end she did not tell the priest. She would keep it to herself and in time, in time, the dream would fade, for it really wasn't a sin, she insisted, and she would forget.

Forget about that young man. Forget about the car hitting him. Forget about her death. *His* death.

She was not in her thirties, but rather sixty-three years of age. Not so young any more. But not so old, either. She had many good years ahead of her. Didn't Sister Catherine say that all the time, and wasn't Sister Catherine—so close to a hundred years now and eighty years a nun—always correct?

Always. Mary Mike would live on and on and on. Forever living.

Until she died, said a small voice, pious in tone. But she shrugged that off.

She had escaped, one part of her said. Escaped from death, glorious death.

Mary Mike shuddered, then hastily crossed herself, and glanced around, as if fearing someone had heard that voice speak.

She walked out to the garden, along a line of trees, and strangely they bothered her. She lowered her eyes until she was past them, and then gingerly dropped to her knees and picked up the trowel from the gardening box she had left it in yesterday . . . a lifetime ago . . . and thrust it into the soil and turned it over, looking at the fat earthworms as they wriggled in the light. She smiled and pulled out the roots of a weed and tossed it into the weed pile.

Behind her the roses nodded in the breeze, and the scent of roses blew on the wind.

She had always been sickly, and was pleased when the nuns took her. She couldn't work long hours, and the Mother knew that, so she had been assigned to the garden because she so enjoyed seeing the plants grow. She sat back and wiped her forehead with the back of her hand, then began troweling again.

She closed her eyes and through the red and amber light saw a hospital room and the starkness of the white walls, and she saw a ring of people standing. Waiting. A death watch.

She frowned, then swiped at a trickle of sweat beading down her cheek.

She worked on and on in the sun, oblivious of the hours, oblivious to her rapid breathing, of the sweat pouring down her forehead and her back now. Worked on and on, because she really must finish working on the herb garden because Mother expected it before the end of July and that was only a few days away. Worked so that she would forget the young man and everything associated with the dream.

Worked and worked until the garden tool dropped from her numbed fingers, worked until the earth whirled around her, and she saw a blue accordion and tubes snaking around and twisting up a tree, and she tumbled forward to lie, her cheek pressed into the soft warm soil, to lie in the sun, to rest just a few minutes, that was all.

To rest. To escape.

She tried to call out, even though speech was forbidden. Tried to, and she shouted and yelled, because this one time she knew they surely wouldn't mind just this one time.

But no one heard. No one came. And finally there was nothing but . . .

Darkness and the smell of roses.

He opened his eyes into the greyness, and he knew he was dead. He had died. Was gone. Passed over. Was no more.

Dust to dust.

He was no longer in the hospital room. But neither was he the young man, nor the old nun.

He was himself, the old man who had fallen from a tree and broken himself into so many pieces that none of the doctors or nurses could put him back together.

He had a great fall.

He had not escaped after all.

He would have laughed . . . had he been able.

The scent of roses was very strong, and he tried to move, but could not. The roses were very close—he realized they had been laid across his chest, and he wrinkled his nose in disgust. He hated their very touch on his cold skin. And distantly, he heard a man's voice droning, and the sounds of sobbing. *Ashes to ashes, dust to dust*, the man was saying.

Dust to dust, the old man thought, and he smiled.

Smiled wildly as the first clod of dirt pelted down upon the coffin.

Smiled and screamed into the greyness, where there was no escape, where he would lay, awake, unable to escape, for all time.

Adrian Cole

ONLY HUMAN

Adrian Cole's most recent novels are the four books in the 'Star Requiem' *series,* Mother of Storms, Thief of Dreams, Warlord of Heaven *and* Labyrinth of Worlds *(published by Unwin Hyman/Grafton). Born in Plymouth, Adrian currently lives in Bideford, Devon, and he has produced several fantasy series since his first short story was published in 1973. Avon has recently reprinted his 'Omaran' saga,* A Place Among the Fallen, Throne of Fools, The King of Light and Shadows *and* The Gods in Anger, *while recent short fiction has appeared in* Dark Voices 2, The Year's Best Fantasy and Horror *and* Fear. *Adrian's latest novel is titled* Blood Red Angel, *and we are pleased to welcome him back to these pages with a humorous reversal of a familiar fantasy theme.*

Swarbang burst through the doors and into the stone chamber as though all the demons in Hell were hot on his tail. Which was an exaggeration, as most of them ignored his passing, as usual. He was not a particularly bright or violent demon himself, but he was nonetheless an ugly brute, capable of chewing the head off a lesser creature of the pantheon if he had to.

A company of his fellows was gathered in the chamber, and as one, they turned their glaring eyes upon the sweating

Swarbang, whose scarlet flesh looked as though it had been roasted over a slow fire.

"It's just as we feared!" he gasped, his long, fat tail slapping the flagstones like an irritated dragon's. "They've got Snagubal. Trapped him!"

The demon conclave—there were a dozen of them— hissed and snarled and generally swore crudely and inventively as only demons can.

Murkrack, largest of them, puffed out his already bloated belly and spat dramatically. "This is insufferable! How *dare* they treat one of us, *us*, Brothers of the Eleventh Grotto, in this way. Intolerable!"

"It's all very well grumbling and spitting and threatening to beat up on the slag imps, Murkrack," snorted the towering Grossbile. "But what in Hell are we going to *do* about it?"

"Do?" snapped Murkrack. "Do? We'll go out there and get him back, that's what!"

"Yes, yes," said Grossbile, looming impatiently. "We know the penalties for not protecting one of our number from sorcery. I'm talking about action. But you haven't properly considered our dilemma. How, precisely, are we supposed to 'go out there' and rescue the hapless Snagubal?"

Murkrack screwed his face up into a hideous mask that made even the demons shudder. "Uh, well . . . we . . . we . . ."

"We can't follow Snagubal," said Grossbile. "He was summoned. By a human sorcerer. Drawn out of our realm to the human world, no doubt to perform some nauseating task to satisfy the whim of the said sorcerer. Unless we are summoned, we can't follow."

"And I've checked carefully," said Swarbang. "The sorcerer who's trapped Snagubal has him in a pentacle."

"Doesn't the idiot know the code for breaking pentacles?" growled Flutterpaddle, a skeletal, green-skinned being with the voice of a constipated frog.

118

"You don't eat me, okay?" (Art: Dave Carson)

"Oh, yes," nodded Swarbang. "But this is a master mage. Snagubal can't move, only to go on errands."

"Which are?"

"Systematically eating certain other sorcerers. Snagubal doesn't mind the odd one or two—who wouldn't?— but too many are bad for the digestion."

"So," snorted Grossbile, "we can't get Snagubal back. Not unless we invoke Under-Devil Zarb, and he'll be so annoyed at Snagubal's incompetence that he'll say the sorcerer is welcome to him!"

"You mean," gulped Swarbang, "that we've lost Snagubal for good? But he's my friend."

Grossbile thought quietly while his companions made more snorting noises. Eventually he hissed for silence. "Ahem! There is a possible solution. We must fight fire with fire. Rather apt, for demons. *We* can't break this pentacle and free Snagubal. Only a human can do that. Very well. We must elicit the aid of a human."

"Won't that be setting a precedent?" grumbled Murkrack.

"I guess so," Grossbile nodded. "But we could draw a pentacle of our own. Humans draw them in their world and summon demons. So why shouldn't we draw one and summon a human? To serve *us*."

The demons gaped, but gradually began to chuckle, then laugh, then roar with mirth, as though they had already accomplished their outrageous plan.

It took considerably longer than they expected, but they finally got their crude pentacle organised. Grossbile had very definite ideas on the shape and most of the sigils, but each of the demons added his own cabalistic marking. They scoured the corridors, holes and burrows of their demonic terrain and assembled a weird assortment of bones, mostly human, a slightly damaged skull, some hanks of hair, and Swarbang's proud contribution—a shrivelled tongue, albeit that of a bovine quadruped.

Scattering these unsavoury items about their pentacle, which they drew in their own blood, they stood outside it in wavering torchlight, waiting to see who would suggest the next move.

"Some sort of chant?" said Flutterpaddle.

"I can't be sure of the words," said Grossbile. "But they should be fairly basic. Let's all hold claws and concentrate."

They did this with some reluctance, not being by nature affectionate creatures, but once Grossbile began his sombre, though fairly convincing chant, they focussed their energy in a combined groaning designed to invoke their human, though Swarbang did wonder if their frightful concatenations would raise the dead.

Around and around the pentacle they shuffled, eyes and teeth gleaming in the torchlight and the air quivered expectantly.

Oliver Firmly was also engaged in a familiar and not dissimilar ritual at this very time, though he was an entire dimension away. He, too, was singing. At least, his attempts at impersonating Pavarotti as he luxuriated in his shower roughly approximated to the equivalent of the bizarre chant in the demons' stone chamber. It may have been his vocal extemporisation on a theme which somehow breached the void, linking him to the utterings of the hideous gathering.

At any rate, he suddenly found himself standing not in his shower, but elsewhere. The soothing hot jet of water had gone. So had most of the lighting. Assuming this to be a power failure, he turned to the glass door of the cubicle, but it was also gone. Only the steam had not completely dissipated, although it had somehow . . . changed. It was more like smoke.

In the absence of the hiss of hot water, Firmly noticed the chanting, or more precisely, croaking, as if a plague of frogs had got loose in the drains. But it couldn't be frogs, it was too harmonious. No, he decided, that wasn't

121

the word. It was horrible.

"I see something!" someone cried, again in batrachian tones.

The smoke cleared a little. Firmly gaped, fingers clutching helplessly at his loofa. He was surrounded by the most horrendous collection of . . . of . . . what in *hell* were they? They looked like escapees from the set of a Cronenberg movie. Jeeze, the *realism*.

"Success!" gurgled another voice. Baleful eyes gleamed. Automatically Firmly swung his loofa to cover the tenderest part of his anatomy.

"What in God's name are you doing in my bathroom?"

"Mind your language!" hissed the tallest of the freaks, his chins wobbling, his vast belly bouncing up and down in the smoke. Something appeared to be keeping both him and his disgusting pink-skinned companions from waddling too close.

"A human," another said.

"Look, will you get the hell out of my goddam bathroom!" shouted Firmly, feeling more than a little ridiculous.

"This is not your world, you repulsive monster," snapped Grossbile, flexing his claws suggestively. "It's *ours*. And if you want to see your world again, you'd better do exactly as you're told. We can easily discard you and summon another one, now that we've mastered the technique."

Firmly shook his head, baffled. But he was in no position to argue. "Look, you guys, will someone tell me what this is all about? I have to be in my office in less than an hour."

Grossbile scratched his chin with an elongated dirk of a fingernail. "Role reversal. We demons have conjured us a human. That is, you."

Firmly nodded slowly. Who were these lunatics?

"One of our colleagues, Snagubal, has been summoned to your world by a particularly ambitious sorcerer, name of Wenceslodin. Snagubal has become an unwilling slave. He can't get back."

122

"It's not fair," whined Swarbang. "He's done what the pact called for, enough maiming and mutilating. But Wenceslodin won't release him."

"You must know this Wenceslodin?" prompted Grossbile.

Firmly swallowed. "Uh—is he some kind of stage magician?"

"Magician, yes. So you do know him?"

"No, not exactly. Who's he with?"

"He is supposed to serve King Urtrabrutes. But he intends to rule your world for himself. He is using Snagubal to eradicate his rivals."

Firmly struggled to keep his composure. They must be fantasy wargamers. That was it. King who? Was there a convention in town?

"The only way we can help Snagubal," Grossbile went on, "is by getting a human to break the pentacle that is his prison. We will gladly send you back to your world. But when you are there, you must free Snagubal."

"How do I do that?"

"Simply break the pentacle. Only a human can do that."

Something clicked in Firmly's mind. He'd never been a great fan of weird fiction, but he seemed to remember a movie once where some kind of demon broke free of its pentacle and *ate* the sap who'd summoned it.

"Hold on, pal. If I break this pentacle, what happens to me? This Snagubal is going to eat me, right?" He shook his head. What am I saying? I'm getting as dumb as these guys! Eat me? Am I kidding?

Swarbang giggled, unable to control himself. "We hadn't thought of that, but he's right."

"We'll just have to make sure Snagubal understands he's being rescued," said Grossbile. "He's reasonably sensible, and should realise. And of course, he's already engorged himself on a dozen or so petty sorcerers. I can't believe he'll still be hungry, pig that he is."

"So all I have to do," said Firmly, "is release your pal, and then I'll be able to get on with my life?"

"Exactly," said Grossbile. "Under such an arrangement there's no need for the usual torture, torment, Hellfire and all that stuff."

"One question."

"Yes?"

"Can I have some clothes?"

The demons screwed up their faces and Firmly gasped in amazement—boy, what they couldn't do with foam latex these days. Really gross stuff.

"Clothes," muttered Grossbile. "I never understood why you humans had to have second skins. We don't bother. Mind you, we do generate a lot more body heat, I suppose."

"We can get him some skins from the flaying caverns," someone suggested.

"I think he wants something more sophisticated," said Grossbile. "Look, you'll have to steal something when you get back. There'll be plenty of clothes in the Tower of Screaming Skulls."

"Excuse me," said Firmly. "Did I hear that right? Skulls?"

"Wenceslodin's retreat. You can pick up some clothes when you get there."

"Can't I just go back to my apartment—"

"No time, no time! Just break the pentacle, that's all. Or do we get ourselves another human?" said Grossbile impatiently, waving his horrendous claws. They, at least, were all too real.

"Okay, okay, let's go for it," groaned Firmly, with as much enthusiasm as a cat about to enter a dog pound.

This time the transition was even more sudden. Like someone had flipped a light switch off. Darkness. Then on again. Poor light, a sort of torchlight? *Torch*light?

Firmly shivered. He really did need clothes. And wherever the hell he was, he needed more than a goddam loofa to defend himself. But curiously enough, the corridor in which he now found himself was lined with shields, undercrossed with swords that gleamed. He had no time to wonder how he had been brought here, though he assumed he'd been drugged in his shower—that smoke beat the heck out of any incense. So now what?

He slipped one of the shields from the wall, but it was far too heavy. He had better luck with the sword. Even so, it was unwieldy.

As he crept down the passage, he wondered how much had been spent on this place. A fortune. This was real stonework. Daylight slatted through a narrow window and he craned his neck to see out. And gaped in disbelief. The landscape of bogs, stunted trees and drifting fog looked like bayou country. If this was some kind of amusement park it was hidden in a part of the city he never heard of. But through a break in the sliding fog he caught a glimpse of distant horizon. The truth hit him at last.

This may be his world, but it sure as heck wasn't his *time*.

Bemused, he went down the corridor and found a spiral stone stair that went up to the higher reaches of the tower. There was nothing else for it; he climbed.

He was panting for breath at the top, where a wooden door barred his way. Cautiously he tried it. It opened. He slipped into the conical chamber. Smoke curled in the air and he could make out a small mountain of clutter in the firelight. This was the magician's den, no doubt about it. There were numerous implements, bones, apparatus, as if this were part chemical plant and part rampant herb garden.

In the centre of the chamber, on the bare wooden floor, was the promised pentacle, sketched with mathematical precision in vivid chalks. And sitting, apparently sleeping, at its heart was a bloated green something, horned and squamous. It could only be Snagubal. One bloodshot eye opened, focusing on Firmly.

He whispered its name and it belched loudly enough to rattle jars on a shelf. The rubbery belly quivered. "Not another task, O great master," the demon moaned.

"I've come to get you out of here."

Something among the clustered shadows by the wall

slithered like a serpent towards the light, rising up and solidifying.

"You're not Wenceslodin," muttered Snagubal, peering at Firmly and wrinkling up his bulbous nose in disgust.

"No," came a withering voice from the shadow-shape as it finished coalescing. "*I* am Wenceslodin." His pale, almost vampiric face was wrapped in a dark hood, deep green eyes fixed on Firmly. A hand rose, a long, pointed finger stabbing out. "Who dares intrude in the Tower of Screaming Skulls? How did you pass the Slavering Guardians?"

Firmly gripped the broadsword tightly, holding it like an overweight fishing rod. "I've come to demand—"

"*Demand*!" snarled the sorcerer, and the air sizzled. "You invite my wrath, you hairless ape!"

"Now hold on, pal," said Firmly, but he could feel the sheer terror groping for his insides like a cold, cold fist. What in God's name was he into here?

"Get back to whatever perverted realm spawned you!" cried Wenceslodin, snapping his fingers. A ball of light zipped across the chamber and clanged against the blade. It was as if an electrical circuit had fused in front of Firmly's face. With a bang and a shower of vivid sparks, the sword flew backwards, almost clipping off an ear.

The blade dug into something by the wall, and there was a flurry of movement overhead. Before Wenceslodin realised what was happening, the cartwheel that had been hoisted up for a chandelier, its securing rope neatly severed, came crashing down. There was another bang, more dramatic sparks, a cloud of smoke, then eventually silence.

Snagubal stood as close as he dared to the inner edge of the pentacle and inspected the ruined heap that was a fusion of wood, metal and sorcerer. He shook his head, jaws wobbling. Firmly took a moment to realise his luck, but then began scrabbling amongst the debris for the cloak. It ripped as he pulled at it, but most of it came free, enough to cover his essentials.

"Don't tell me," moaned Snagubal, with another volcanic belch. "You want me to devour your enemies."

As he spoke, the rubble moved and a bony arm reached out and, crab-like, clawed the splintered wood away. Wenceslodin was evidently far from deceased. Firmly swung round on Snagubal.

"Come on, we're leaving."

"Leaving?"

"Going back to your cronies." Firmly bent down and prepared to wipe away part of the pentacle with his makeshift garment. "But get one thing straight. You don't eat me, okay? YOU DO NOT EAT ME. I'll get you back and you send me home, that's the deal."

Snagubal nodded vigorously. Firmly broke the pentacle and at once Snagubal leapt free of it, shrieking with triumph. His long claws locked on Firmly's wrist and his mouth opened to reveal a surprising number of pointed teeth.

"I just ate," he said. "But later—"

He was interrupted by a howl of anger as the rubble burst to reveal the re-forming shape of Wenceslodin. Firmly felt himself tugged off his feet, the demon's grip like fire. He plunged once more into total darkness.

"A close call." Firmly was sitting, dazed, in the centre of the pentacle the demons had drawn for him. In the sulphurous smog, he could see their gargoyle-like faces studying him. Snagubal was among them, glowering in an exasperated way, as if annoyed at being deprived of a potential human meal.

Something moved behind the crowding demons, a blood-red form. Its eyes were like coals, its skin deep red, and as it pushed the demons contemptuously aside they bowed reverentially before it.

"Under-Devil Zarb," someone murmured. Silence clamped down.

The satanic figure studied Firmly, lifting a fat scroll. "You are the human, Oliver Firmly." It was like a sentence of death.

Firmly nodded. His body had begun to shiver and he pulled the tattered cloak more tightly around him.

"I understand," went on Under-Devil Zarb, "that these imbeciles summoned you in order to rescue Snagubal. A matter I will be dealing with in due course."

"We struck a bargain," said Firmly, voice quaking.

"So I gather. And our Principal is very particular about honouring bargains. Lucky for you. You wish to return to your world?"

Firmly nodded.

Zarb consulted the scroll. "That won't be possible. In view of what has happened, certain complications have arisen in the continuum. Matrix warping and so on. In short, your world no longer exists."

"*What!*"

"Events in the Tower of Screaming Skulls so tangled the time mandalas that your world just—dissipated."

Firmly got a grip on his tottering senses. "Wait a minute. That wasn't my world. Not where I *came* from, anyhow."

Zarb frowned, again studying the scroll. "This information is accurate. Ah, but wait. I should have known! Trust these fools to botch things! It was one of a number of alternative realities. I see your own world diverged from that of ex-sorcerer Wenceslodin at a given point."

"So can I go back now?"

"Hmm." Zarb shook his head. "Still impossible. According to this, you've died. Heart attack. While having a shower. Disgusting practice. No wonder your heart gave out."

Firmly felt himself going faint. His mouth opened and closed, but he couldn't speak.

There was a minor altercation and a winged creature flapped to Zarb's side, waving another, thinner parchment. Zarb took it irritably, eyes scanning its contents.

"I see. An update. The time mandalas have been even more distorted by your erratic movements than was first realised."

"So am I dead . . . or what?"

"It appears not. Your summoning here actually altered your world, or to be more precise, the path of your own existence."

"Then—"

"You missed the coordinate of your death. So you can go back to a much longer life span. Your new time of death will be—"

"*Don't tell me*! I don't want to know!"

"Really? Humans usually offer up their souls for such information. Still, a bargain is a bargain—"

"Right now, all I want is to get back and finish my shower in peace."

"Very well. But do you mind if I give you a word of advice? No more singing. Not if you value your freedom."

"On my soul. But let's make this a gentleman's agreement, huh? No more bargains."

Trevor Donohue and Paul Collins

UNNAMED

Trevor Donohue was born in Tasmania and has published a dozen or so short stories, mostly in collaboration with Paul Collins. His first novel, Savage Tomorrow, *was well received in Australia and a second full-length work,* The Road to Tiger Park, *is currently being serialised in the Australian magazine* Interstater. *Paul Collins was born in Essex, but he currently lives in Brisbane, Queensland. Australia's most published living SF and fantasy author, Paul is also the editor of five anthologies of antipodean science fiction and a "Best of" collection was published by Wilhelm Goldmann in Germany. They both make their debut in* Fantasy Tales *with the offbeat story which follows . . .*

I came into existence. Nightmares became pain and with pain I awoke in the moist, clinging twilight.

I had no clue as to my past, who I was, or where. I found myself naked and unadorned, spreadeagled. Beneath me vibrated, fluctuated, a gently, pulsing floor. I floated, suspended above a circle of darkness.

Around the perimeter of the circle, another great circle of multi-coloured mosaics, a wonderful shifting kaleidoscope of predominantly greenish hues.

Above me a brilliant red cavern, translucent, a diffused sunset with traceries of frozen blue lightning.

Where was I? How long would my nightmare last? Dim memories struggled, trying to reach my level of consciousness. If only I could break out and find some clue to my forced incarceration.

I struggled upright. The floor sucked at my feet, preventing movement. I persevered, fell, regained my balance, toppled once more. Then I lay quite still and allowed the writhing floor to caress me.

Then unexpectantly a great tear in the ceiling expanded vertically and slowly folded back, to fall away like a great velvet curtain.

Then the chamber was flooded with blinding light, its source a brightly burning sun that threatened all life within the cavern.

As the aperture widened I became aware of movement immediately above me.

Great God the imagination knows no bounds! I *felt* the binding morass that was my prison, could *smell* the heavy odour of blood, and now knew fear, *real* fear as rumblings echoed from beyond the cavern.

From tiny points within the wall's structure there appeared multi-clawed abominations such as only Poe or Lovecraft could ever conceive. They wormed their way through the wall, and with their tentacles leading their hideous shapes they clawed forward.

A subliminal thought offered knowledge: Demodices. Somehow I knew what they were yet I had never before encountered them.

Lacking a fuller understanding of this paradox, I crouched down and hugged the floor to avoid their weaving insidious heads that moved restlessly, almost blindly.

They appeared to be agitated by my presence, yet they made no immediate assault upon my person. Could they smell me? Surely they must discover my position at any moment!

Fear and panic made me scramble madly about, forced me

Within the wall's structure there appeared multi-clawed abominations.
(Art: Allen Koszowski)

to run blindly so much so that I rather slid from place to place, and splashed across the small confines in which I had been incarcerated.

Then to my horror a wave of warm, glutinous fluid swept across the cavern floor, a monstrous torrent that bore me past my adversaries and expelled me outwards.

Out of my prison I tumbled and downwards into an alien landscape, finally to leave me pummeled and bruised, gasping for breath.

The tidal wave was now nothing more than a trickle, the remnants of which began to solidify, forcing me to move quickly before I could become embedded in its cooling, hardening embrace.

My new surroundings were in vast contrast to those I had previously encountered. This outer world was pitted and sectioned in a regular manner that suggested that at one time there had been a crude form of agriculture. And in the distance there rose a mountainous range.

Judging by the warmth beneath my feet I judged those towering rocks to be of volcanic temperament. Now also there was a strong gravitational pull in the lesser atmosphere and surface particles dislodged by my feet began to drift upwards like minute motes.

Gradually I gained knowledge through comparison. This world had a different gravity from what I vaguely knew in another existence.

Cautiously at first, then with greater confidence, I progressed with giant steps, setting a pace that I guessed would have once been beyond me.

Several times in the far distance I glimpsed other lifeforms not at all belonging to the world which I dimly recalled.

The terrain began to change—the rough fields ran into a gnarled and petrified forest: one immense surreal woodland devoid of foliage: death represented upon each quivering branch.

It was here I discovered the body. A decapitated corpse, one partly disemboweled. Yet in spite of my repugnance I forced myself to examine the cadaver, to perhaps find some clue to my own identity. Surely I might salvage something from the remains? On closer inspection I felt disturbed that perhaps I had known the dead person. A friend? Had we arrived together and been separated by a wave?

Someone not long dead. By the contusions and cuts, the head had apparently been severed by a pincer motion that had closed inwards then torn out the man's throat.

Anxiously then I cast a quick glance to ensure my privacy. It must have been a formidable creature to inflict such damage. Then all at once I was moving. A flurry of movement to my left had erupted without warning. From behind a gently pulsating mound I scanned my surroundings.

It was another man. Flailing his arms as though in sheer terror, his features stamped with fear. Some of his panic took grip of me and I nearly joined him in his exodus. But caution made me wary in these unfamiliar surroundings, and I sadly let the stranger pass without attracting his attention.

The man's passing presaged imminent danger.

So I remained hidden, almost content to learn there were others of my ilk, no matter how endangered a species we might be.

As with that poor wretch I had discovered earlier, there was a persistent premonition that these men were known to me. His build and facial outline were too familiar, yet my subconscious denied my conscious thirst for knowledge.

So here I waited, secure for the moment that at least I had remained hidden from one man, which implied my sanctuary would hide me from others.

The temperature here remained constant. I now also noted with unease that the sun had not moved in all the time I had been here.

Again there was movement in the distance, and when the figure came into sight I recognised him as being the same tortured man who had recently fled past me.

Had he blundered, thereby losing his way to retrace his earlier steps? Without noticeable landmarks had he become disoriented, to remain no nearer escape from the terror that pursued him?

Uneasily I allowed him to pass without offering assistance. Again I waited. There was more movement, a stumbling figure emerged. It was the same man again. Impossible: there had been no time for him to backtrack. Again I let him pass.

Seconds of silence until that same nightmarish intruder rushed past me to be swallowed by the darkness to my right.

Again and again and again.

Soon I became claustrophobic. I was captured in a single sequence, forced to watch a repetitive re-enactment of the same event.

Again the sound of someone approaching, a difference, a more intense suggestion of movement. Then there were two of them, each a duplicate of the other, and both running side by side.

Running from who? Running from what?

It was then that a chill, a tremor of premonition coursed through my veins. I knew then that they were me, I was they. I had been observing my own doppelgängers.

There had been a transition in time and substance, but not as I had calculated in distance. I had not been transported onto an alien world, but rather absorbed into an inner world, one familiar yet fantastically foreign. I had been absorbed into *myself*.

I recognised the demons for what they were. *Folliculus Daemoniacus*: those minute organisms that live in one's eyelashes.

I had wakened in the pupil of my own eyeball.

Memory slowly returned and with it came excruciating pain. Mental anguish, vastly removed from physical suffering.

I knew my identity. I was, *had* been, a writer, more specifically a master of prolific absurdities. A literary man damned, one with feet of clay creating hurdles to leap, trying to bottle the sun and refusing to rest in the shade—absolute motion going nowhere—one hand clapping, the other juggling, trying to view the moon through a milk bottle, a scorpion stinging itself.

Living a lifestyle where love and hate became synonymous with pleasure and pain, the latter dominating.

Creative yet believing in nothing: never seeking or finding friends.

A lifestyle as barren as the plain through which I had trekked, as stark as the forest where I dwelled. A journey down the contours of my own face into the stubble of my beard.

My last conscious thought had been looking into the bore of a pistol, knowing my finger was drawing tight on the trigger, unable to resist the temptation to end my existence. And feeling at once euphoric now that I was about to exit from a world to which I had never contributed.

Now I knew my destiny: to be alone after all, prey to organisms that live within man's mortal body.

The overhead sun was an electric light globe.

Somebody please turn out the light . . .

Phillip C. Heath

BAG OF BONES

Phillip C. Heath's fiction last appeared in Fantasy Tales *back in
1982. He lives in Florida and has contributed stories to several
genre magazines, including* Whispers, The Horror Show,
Eldritch Tales *and* Gothic. *His work has been anthologised
in* The Year's Best Horror Stories, Nightmares 2 *and* 3,
Horrorstory, The Fontana Book of Great Ghost Stories
and The Fontana Book of Great Horror Stories. *He is
currently working on a novel, a long-term project for him.
We welcome Phillip back to these pages with this ghoulish yarn
about a bodysnatcher.*

Whether accident led to curiosity I cannot say. Perhaps I
should confess to the contrary. Whatever the case, it was
a damning combination of circumstance. Admittedly, I was
already having some misgivings about the whole thing as the
carriage drew nearer our destination. The night was black as
sin, and a prowling autumn wind moved all alone through the
quiet streets. There was a cold, heavy sinking in my stomach as
I dwelled bitterly on such miserable misfortune as had brought
me to this.

Only six months ago a well-to-do upperclassman in medicine
at Cambridge University, I had been formally accused of
stealing and trafficking dangerous drugs from the supply

storerooms. It was a vicious falsehood, of course—the real guilty party averted suspicion from themselves by instead cleverly victimizing me. I must say they could be commended for a job well done, too, for shortly thereafter I was expelled and an ugly public scandal ensued. Disgraced, family and friends outwardly shunning me, now the proverbial black sheep, and hence I had no alternative but to leave home with a curse on the entire medical profession burning upon my lips.

Forced to seek other employ, I might easily have starved to death or perished in debtor's prison had I not one dreary day in my desperate wanderings happened upon that certain sign down Seymour Place, betwixt a tobacconist's and hatter's shop, in Paddington, West London. The black lettering read:

JEREMY SLOAN
UNDERTAKER

—All Orders Promptly Attended To—
—A Good Hearse Kept For Hire—
—Winding Sheets, Shrouds, and Coffins—
Kept on Hand or Made to Order
—Agent For Gravestones—

At first the proprietor turned me away also, until I pressed my sad story upon him and explained my present lot. He somehow seemed to sympathize, admired my candour, and quickly took a liking to me. Ere long I was a familiar figure about the place, helping him in general with his business and conducting various duties. And being paid well for it.

But then he came to me with an odd request. Several very old and rather expensive family heirlooms had been stolen from the premises, said he, and were being ransomed for their safe recovery. He wanted them back and was indeed willing to pay, though fearful to retrieve them in person as the exchange was to

140

"*I have reserved the empty niche over there for him.*" (Art: Alan Hunter).

be made at a nefarious alehouse in a treacherous section of the East End. Might I go in his stead?—there would be a generous bonus for my trouble . . .

I looked up from my brooding and became aware that the vehicle had abruptly come to a halt. I leaned out.

"This 'ere's as far as I go, mate," the cabby announced. "Bad place, this." He studied me curiously for a moment. "But I s'pose you know thet."

I stepped down and handed him the fare.

"Thankin' you, sir," he muttered, smiling thinly, whereupon he reined the horse around and with a clop and clatter swiftly vanished into the gloom.

I turned up my collar against the night's chill breath and stuck both hands in the pockets of my coat, remembering reluctantly the advice that I best wear as plain and inconspicuous dress as possible. Then I crossed over to Flower and Dean Street.

The area hereabout was a squalid and disease-ridden labyrinth of passages, lanes, courtyards, and vile housing, all overcrowded with countless unemployed poor—the warren of a motley collection of wastrels, whores, brigands, and cutthroats. Empty ruins of many demolished buildings evidenced progress of the railway companies, and there was not a solitary gaslight on any of the street corners, making the careless passer-by all the more vulnerable. A terribly melancholy, helpless feeling seized me. Truth to tell, for a while I seriously contemplated turning back, but finally determined to hurry and be done with it. The sooner away from this cheerless place, the better.

Presently I espied the weathered, decrepit sign which hung askew before one of the grimy buildings: DRAGON'S DEN, it said.

Once more I hesitated. "Enquire for a man named Hooks," I had been told. "Ask him no questions, and be wary of watching eyes. He will give you a parcel of some sort; take it and begone straight-away." Gathering my courage, I entered.

It was a noisy, disgusting hellhole of ruffians and vagabonds, spectral shapes shrouded in a thick, blue pall of smoke; cheap tallow candles guttered fitfully, casting sooty scraps of shadow here and there. An uncomfortable number of malign and hungry-looking eyes immediately fell upon me. Awkwardly I began to move across the tap room, trying my best not to draw unnecessary attention, and edged up to the bar so that my back was toward the wall. I motioned for who I took to be the servingwoman, an ancient crone with spidery wisps of hair and eyes like dirty coins.

"Excuse me. I—I'm hunting for a chap named Hooks," I explained.

"Wot fer?" she croaked, her tongue roaming between four crooked, tombstone teeth.

"He is expecting me."

After a thoughtful pause she wordlessly lifted a gnarled finger to indicate a table in one of the more darksome corners of the tavern.

"Hooks?" I asked of the person seated there, with strained composure.

A scarecrow of a man wearing a tattered, filthy, food-stained shirt lazily looked up. He coughed phlegm and spat on the floor, only inches from my boot. "You from the dismal trader?"

"Beg your pardon?"

He sneered at my irksome ignorance. "You know, the bleedin' undertaker."

I nodded that I was and sat down.

"Do you-uh-have something for me?"

"All fit 'n' proper."

His voice lowered. "But not 'ere. Outside, in the buildin' 'round back. Wait a wink afore you follow." He cautiously glanced around, then slipped through the rear entrance and was gone. Out of the corner of my eye several menacing figures skulked closer.

I delayed perhaps a full minute before heading anxiously toward the door. Two rat-faced boys eyed me on the way out, doubtless wondering if this nervous stranger carried anything worth slitting a throat for. Evidently they thought not, since fortunately none engaged in pursuit.

I crept along the muddy, uncobbled alley to a decaying tenement, loitered uneasily there in the foul-smelling hallway for the thief to appear. Beneath the staircase a half dead, gin-sodden wretch lay tossing feverishly in his sleep. In one of the open rooms a few doors down I could overhear a young harlot entertaining her customer.

At length the man returned from upstairs with a bound, soiled sackcloth clutched tightly in one hand. The other he extended greedily.

I surrendered a dozen gold sovereigns and he snatched them up, testily bit one, and thrust the bag in my face. Heeding the instructions given me earlier, I turned to make haste.

Suddenly there was a great guffaw. "Madman: Beetle-headed fool."

Startled, I looked back. "What do you mean by that?"

He met my frown with an oafish grin. "'Oo else in 'is flippin' roight mind would stump up good money for an arm full o'—" He caught himself. "Ah, but mum's the word, eh? Heh, heh, 'Ooks knows when to kape 'is yap shut. You tell yer man that, lad." He clacked the coins in the palm of his hand. "Yessir, any ol' time 'Ooks can be o' service . . ." He cackled again, then retreated into the black confines of the dwelling whence he came.

As luck would have it, I was able to get clear of the district lacking further adventure, and once beyond the slum gratefully hailed a cab which delivered me safely back to Seymour Place and familiar surroundings. Yet it seemed this dark drama had just begun. For, as I alighted from the conveyance, the thin material of the bag was accidently caught upon a sharp protuberance of the door latch, and torn. A sizeable hole resulted. Consequently, when the coach departed down the way, I obeyed a natural impulse and stepped to the nearest streetlight to quite innocently examine its contents. I should not have done so.

Therein, I found not cherished keepsakes, no, but a large number of—*bones*. Human bones.

I was aghast. My initial shock gave way to an unsuppressed shudder, then something akin to indignation. Had I put myself in peril for naught but a few crumbling old bones? I dare say Hooks was right: my employer was surely not possessed of all his senses. Heirlooms indeed: still other thoughts scuttered across my mind. Why had he plainly lied to me? In order that I might wilfully do his bidding, obviously; though how could he have ever succumbed to such an outlandish plot? And anyway, what would he possibly want with them in the first place?

I closed up the sack and admitted myself into the mortuary.

Perhaps, I decided, I was letting my imagination get the better of me, and merely jumping to conclusions. It was a strange thing, to be sure, but could he not have *some* logical explanation for it all?

Yes, probably he did, although I was never enlightened as to what that might be. He was there waiting when I arrived, and our midnight rendezvous was brief. I gave him the bundle, he gladly relieved me of it, and without further ado politely sent me on my way. The next day no mention was made regarding the bag nor its cryptic contents. Henceforth neither did I remark on the subject myself, as I thought it best to remain reserved in my veritable ignorance of the matter. Such reticence did not, however, so readily dispel the lingering disquietude of that peculiar night. But eventually other demands upon my attention prevailed elsewhere, and, in time, it was more or less forgotten.

Two months quickly came and went. During this passage we were kept busy with an increasing number of jobs, many of them brought about by an erratic outbreak of typhus, presumably spread by rodents or seepage from infectious churchyard graves into the city water supplies. Too, the impassive Thames contributed several of her more recent victims—"floaters", as Mr Sloan called them—and for a while gunpowder was left burning nightly so as to mask the insufferable stench of their rapid decomposition. Usually if there was to be some delay the bodies we received were temporarily preserved in ice, and embalming performed in those instances when required or requested.

Although my field of learning did prove advantageous, my own duties were of course primarily custodial; arranging the folding chairs, taking charge of pallbearers, assisting in the loading and removal of the coffin from the hearse, and running whatever routine errands my employer would have me do. Similarly, he supplied the casket, obtained the permit, paid the church sexton for bell tolling and grave digging, and by and large saw to any other chief concerns until the deceased was lowered, when customarily adding a few shillings to his bill for being in attendance.

Remuneration for such services ranged from ten pounds in the case of the average funeral to as much as fifty or sixty for what was privately referred to as "all the trimmings". And it is interesting to note that whereas the majority of those in our profession those days were comparatively hard pressed and looked upon as merchants of a rather grubby order, preying shrewdly on grief, remorse, and guilt, Mr Jeremy Sloan managed to lift himself above this distasteful stigma, whatsoever its justification. Having come unexpectedly into a somewhat substantial inheritance, he had been in the position to build up his business over the years to attract especially people of wealth, prominence, and fashion. And though I suppose one could not slight him for that, I occasionally wondered about the nature of this inheritance, particularly considering his guarded manner with reference to his past. But then, it was probably none of my affair.

One cloudy afternoon when we had finished up a trifle early, he unceremoniously bade me join him for some sherry, and to discuss a certain, urgent "business matter" which necessitated

146

our deliberation. A ripple of restlessness passed through me. It was true that of late I noticed he acted singularly distraught, as if something profound or oppressive weighed on his mind. Indeed, apparently, this was now about to be disclosed.

I followed him into the parlour, a small room tastefully furnished in upholstered walnut and rosewood, conveying an appropriate air of darkness and dignity. Here he procured two tall-stemmed glasses and poured from a delicate decanter. We each settled back into a chair.

For many long moments my host remained silent, a tall, sombre figure neatly attired in his usual stern greys and blacks, face creased with concern.

Finally he looked up from his drink. "My young friend," he began, measuring his words pensively, "deeply am I disheartened, and come to seek solace in your kind assistance concerning the situation—one which obligates my good conscience to approach you thus. But permit me to explain.

"No doubt you have heard of the notorious Saint Mary's of Bethlehem, in Lambeth?"

I nodded that I had.

"Well, recently I happened to learn an old associate of mine has been 'residing' there for some time, unbeknownst to myself and what other personal acquaintances he may have had. He was always a rather wayward sort of individual, no family ties, few friends, and—" He exhaled raggedly and shifted in his seat. "But these particulars are of little significance. The issue at hand is to get him out. He is only an old man, you see, a mite addled perhaps, but perfectly harmless; and it grieves me sorely to envision him in that—place. No, I cannot just leave him there to waste away . . . and this is the reason you must help me."

I still did not quite understand. "But why? Could you not petition his release, have him entrusted to your custody?"

He shook his head forlornly. "Would that it was so easy. *'Lasciate ogni speranza voi ch'entrate'*. Nay, there is but one way to free him from his fate—escape."

When I started to object he anticipated it and confidently raised a hand for silence. "Hearken carefully now, for I have a plan . . ."

And so he did. And so also was I very much surprised to find myself listening attentively, obediently, even in light of my previous experience which kindled further doubts.

Yet he made it sound so simple.

"So all you have to do," he was saying, "is meet one of the nightwatchmen tomorrow evening at the rear entrance. Alfred Cobbs is his name. He shall be expecting you, and knows my instructions. Follow him and do exactly as he tells you. I believe he can be trusted well enough, but take care as he is not of an exceptionally humorous disposition, and somewhat of a queer duck himself. However, he has already been paid half of what was promised him, and even that a sight more than the handful of coppers he secretly charges for admissions. There should be no difficulty, since supervision as a whole is normally not very strict.

"I fully realize the import of what I ask, but stand you so assured you, too, shall be paid most handsomely. Of course I would undertake this business myself, but the place depresses me so, and at any rate, I would only get in the way of things. So be of keen eye and tarry not; fetch him directly hither to me where I will be waiting."

He must have read the befuddled, reluctant look on my face, for he leaned closer toward me. His voice was grave, his breath seeming to smell faintly of funeral flowers.

"Please, I implore, you must do this—for my friend. For me. What say you?"

I gazed helplessly into the haunted and uneasy flickering deep in his eyes, and gave him my answer.

As I was told, every detail had been carefully seen to well in advance. Precisely at midnight a brougham showed up in front of my flat. The featureless, dolefully-dressed coachman was silent as a pallbearer, and uttered nary a word as I climbed inside and the vehicle lurched forward. Most likely his musings were on his bulging purse.

A light but steady rain had fallen shortly after dusk, and the storm wandered off on lightning legs. We struck southward past Marble Arch and Hyde Park, then crossed Westminster Bridge to the east, keeping as much as possible to the more deserted back streets, winding through tortuous, ill-lit avenues and byways, their narrow walks packed with garbage and trash.

New apprehensions, like the dampness outside, sent a chill creeping up my legs. All the day long I had been regretfully mulling over the precipitated sentiment of my decision, and now could only reflect on the unsettling tales I heard regarding these so-called "hospitals for the insane"—notably the infamous Saint Mary's of Bethlehem, commonly known as simply Bedlam, a degeneration of "Bethelehem" and an association for the uproar behindst its walls. Mediaeval views held that all forms of dementia were caused by evil spirits and witchcraft, and so burned at the stake those possessed; then the populace concluded lunacy was not only incurable but catching as well, and thence conveniently shut them away to suffer under the brutal and inhuman treatment meted out by their callous, drunken attendants. To be shamefully exhibited to the curious and whipped regularly to control their frenzy, but verily more for the sadistic pleasure of visitors. No, it would not be pleasant.

We turned down St Georges Road and in due course found ourselves approaching the bleak, desolate stone structure that reared up ominously in the night. The driver pulled around the rear and located a spot to wait quietly in one of the vaster shadows. I slipped out and hurried through the kitchen garden to the massive oaken door as described to me earlier. Swallowing dryly, I knocked thrice.

There was the rattling of latchkey in lock, and the door abruptly opened inward with a groan. A foreboding silhouette stood at its threshold.

"Well?" Two piercing eyes regarded me.

"M-Mr. Sloan sent me. I—"

A huge, pawlike hand grabbed my collar and drew me inside. Alfred Cobbs was something to make one lie awake nights. Although his hair hung in his eyes, one of them was grotesquely bloodshot—noticeably more so than the other; tobacco spittle rimmed his lower lip and had dried in the red whiskers of his thin, unkempt beard, and he smelled like a goat. He also bore the distinct scars of human bite marks on his left forearm.

"Foller me," he grunted, and led the way down a dim corridor. We passed through the ward for noisy male patients, a lengthy gallery of rooms on either side. Several of the doors stood ajar, permitting a passing glance at the deplorable conditions therein. The lice-infested cubicles were exceedingly cramped, and the heating inadequate. Ghastly moans, howls, wails, and giggling stirred the hairs on the back of my neck, echoing in the unseen distance. But what was most appalling was the pitiful semblance of humanity I glimpsed inside: bruised, sore-encrusted faces contorted in perpetual grimaces of terror, anguish, rage, or despair—pale forms scurrying about like gaunt, starving rats. But not all enjoyed such liberties; over here was a slobbering cripple, legs securely bound, arms strapped to his sides; yonder a young idiot girl in shackle and chains, slowly dying from rickets.

We proceeded through the keeper's quarters and the cold bathrooms, then slipped out a door and traversed the vacant yard which served as one of the open airing grounds reserved for specific inmates. On the opposite side lay the cell block used to house the more violent, criminal patients, and once within headed down another drafty hallway. The wolfish turnkey conducted me past an intersecting passage, of a sudden stopping to open the closest door on the right. Then, to both my astonishment and horror, he shoved me inside. Before I could turn around the door slammed with a frightful finality. The sound of his quick footsteps and coarse laughter faded off down the hall, and everything grew still.

In frantic desperation I clamorously beat, wrenched, and clawed at the door, yet all in vain; it was locked tight as a crypt, nor did anyone heed my repeated cries for help. I had been betrayed, left alone to what denouement I dared not dwell upon.

But no, it seemed I was not unaccompanied in my plight, for as I struggled to assemble my thoughts a dry, wheezy voice drifted through the gloom. "Your pleas fall on deaf ears, my son. Soon you will feel the strain of remaining sane. For is not sanity merely the folds in the lids of divine eyes whose bounds cannot be held?—the phantom that only a supreme sense can envisage, and the yearning of they who cannot be seen?"

I spun around and peered into the dark corners of the room. A detestable odour arose with the faint rustling from somewhere nearby.

"W-Who's there?" I ventured. A haggard, wizened little man shuffled forward into the single crack of light filtering in from some outside source. His hair was long, white, and disheveled, ensnarled with specks of straw. "Your lesson," he intoned solemnly, "should be clear: Do not turn to mediums or wizards; do not seek them out to be defiled by them, for I am the Lord your God."

"Stay away from me," I cautioned, hoarsely.

All at once his eyes were a wild thing's, wide and staring as if they might pop out. He pointed an accusing finger. "You! . . . You are one of *them*!" The vein-rutted hands made weird gestures, and he commenced to chant. "Black-luggie, hammer-head, Rowan-tree and red-thread. Put the warlocks to their speed!"

His brain had gone rotten, like an egg.

"Off with you spirits of Fear, spirits of Doom! Give way to the sun and the moon, for this is a sanctuary, this a place made safe. Blessings and peace, blessings and peace."

The raving creature bent down and picked up a dagger-like shard of broken pottery, twisting his head from side to side like some moronic monkey. He slowly moved closer. "And I

151

said unto you, 'Thou shalt not suffer a witch to live. Whosoever lieth with the serpent shall surely be put to death. And he that sacrificeth unto any god save the Lord only, shall be utterly destroyed' . . ."

Trembling in every limb, I backed up against the door—when suddenly it opened wide and a hand yanked me into the corridor. The door was slammed shut.

Alfred Cobbs stood grinning at me—the leer of a gargoyle.

"Weè bit scairt, were ye?"

"What was the meaning of that outrage?" I demanded furiously.

He wiped his nose with the back of his dirty shirt sleeve.

"The 'ead warder was comin', so I 'ad to 'ide ye. Heh, don't wanna get caught now, do ye?"

I believed it more of a malicious jest, but said nothing and continued to glare at him.

"C'mon," he ordered. Grudgingly I followed.

Five doors down he paused, and held out his palm.

"This 'ere's the one. Let's see it."

I reached in my cloak and extracted a small pouch of coins. I demurred, my wrath still smouldering.

"Very well," I replied with reckless bravado, "but first I must tell you, sir, that you are a scoundrel, and quite frankly I find your manners and misconduct positively atrocious."

For an instant his expression hardened with more than a subtle suggestion of cruelty, then he looked me over most strangely and moistened his lips.

"Takes a rightly big man to speak them kind o' words," he smirked, pocketing his prize. "I only 'opes yer big enough to 'andle the likes of this 'ere deranged lunatic."

He obviously derived great pleasure from intimidating me.

"How-How do you mean?" I asked.

He withdrew a ring of passkeys from his trousers and inserted one of them into the lock. "S'nothin', really," turning it. "Jist don't know too much about this blighter—one o' them sly, quiet birds. Never know what to 'spect till they creeps up b'hind ye and—*Gaghh*!" He throttled an invisible throat.

The door swung open.

"You!" growled the gaoler. "Get out 'ere."

An old, rather brutish hulk of a man in threadbare clothes groped his way into the light. Then I realized he was completely blind, his eyes sunken, empty pits, and his face hideously disfigured. "Yer goin' on the outside with this feller," the other informed him gruffly, tying his wrists. "Keep still and don't be waggin' yer tongue any—'ear?" The man nodded slowly.

Cobbs led us around the corner and up to a window we were to climb out, from which the bars had been removed. He offered no assistance in helping wrestle the big man through but simply stood there glowering at me. Then he said, in a low, snaking whisper, "Don't wanna ever set eyes on yer wormy 'ide again, boy, or I'll be spittin' on yer carcass."

He turned and was gone.

Once outside I made haste with my consort to the awaiting coach, wherein we speedily departed, eager to be far-removed from that horrid madhouse, and the queer beast named Cobbs.

Darkness lay over the world like a coffin lid and a ghostly fog had settled in, gathering in little wreaths and eddies like some pale, sluggish monster. The stranger beside me remained silent, as he was told, undoubtedly aware that someone intentionally arranged to have him secreted out. But the whole time I also could not forget the guard's spiteful warning, and nervously wondered if my employer had correctly assessed the character of his friend.

When the conveyance wheeled up behind the mortuary I flipped open my pocket-watch. It was well after three o'clock.

Mr Sloan met us anxiously at the door, but hardly had I taken off my cloak when he was ushering me back out again.

"I cannot express to you the extent of my gratitude," he confided. "And as a modest favour in return I shan't request that you come in to-morrow. Sleep, rest. Good night."

Suddenly I was all alone on the steps. I had started to walk away until I remembered having left my hat and gloves on one of the chairs. I went back to the door, but found it already locked. Flustered, I used my own key and entered. No one was in sight, though I heard muffled voices coming from the reposing room. Something struck me as somehow odd about it, and so I peeked inside.

The place was empty.

But nonetheless I overheard a most peculiar conversation: "Well, Mr Black, you certainly look for the worst since last I saw you. I scarcely thought it possible."

"Where am I? 'Oo are you?"

"Why, sweet William, has it really been so long? Pray tell, do you not know your old friend, Jeremy Sloan?"

Then there was a scuffling noise, a painful gasp, and heavy thud. After that, a sinister stillness.

I left quietly and hurried home. My harrowing ordeal had left me thoroughly exhausted, and yet, I could not sleep.

Early the next morning I visited the local library and delved through some dated copies of the *East London Advertiser*. Something was gnawing at my memory, a half-forgotten tale I vaguely recollected from my boyhood days. Finally I found it. I fell to further pondering as a definite dread ran icy fingers down my spine, and somehow knew it was too late to disentangle myself from this web of mystery.

Shortly after midday I returned to the mortuary and let myself in, briefly noting that the windows were fast drawn and shuttered. A sullen hush hung in the air. No one was about.

Moving quietly through the entrance hall, I once again stepped into the reposing room, and began to rummage around. Within a few minutes I had confirmed my speculations, discovering a hidden panel in the wall behind some dusty draperies and a large candelabra. I experimentally exerted pressure at one side, and it creaked open onto a short flight of stone steps leading down to a black,

154

sepulchral recess—wherefrom the voices came the night before.

Stealthily, with oil-lamp and much trepidation, I descended the stairs and found myself in a small preparation room, part of what at one time served as a mouldering wine cellar, now converted for some unknown purpose into a dank, musty retreat. There were numerous shelves recently built along one of the walls, filled to capacity with scalpels, scissors, forceps, pumps, clamps, and other such paraphernalia, together with an extensive array of fluids, powders, oils and pastes. A shuddersome assortment of medical curiosities slumbered in milky jars of formaldehyde. Near these were a basin and ewer atop a tiny washstand, freshly filled with water, and beside that a darkly-stained smock on a hook.

But there was still more. A long, wooden laying-out board upon which a suggestively-shaped object had been covered with a sheet.

Swallowing the cold tightness in my throat, I reached over and jerked away the linen.

It was the naked body of the inmate whom I had brought from Bedlam.

Standing there aquiver, I gaped at the dead man before me, alive only yestereve. It looked as if he had been struck hard across the forehead with a blunt instrument. All his blood was drained out through the carotid artery, and a trocar—a long, hollow needle attached to a tube—had been jabbed into the abdomen and chest cavity to remove the contents, which was to be replaced with a chemical solution.

I covered the poor devil back up and eased through the thin curtain partition into the larger chamber beyond.

What met my eyes froze the very marrow in my bones. It was like something out of a nightmare. The room was round, about thirteen feet in diameter. A small sconce flickered feebly, eerily revealing several niche-like hollows carved in the wall at intervals, each inset with a single piece of protective glass. And every case, save one, displayed its own abomination.

The long-dead remains of four corrupted but partially preserved corpses, each painstakingly posed. Parchment-coloured flesh shriveled tightly over bone, as if plucked from their graves and hung here to dry, nostrils flared, eyeless sockets staring, jaws wide, forever screaming—or laughing. Two, however, were nothing more than skeletons, one fully clothed and wearing a worn cap, a leathery length of cord draped between its outstretched hands.

Just then, as I was about to fly the place in horror, there was the soft tread of a footstep behind me. I whirled.

Mr Sloan stood by the curtain smiling smugly.

He brought forth a folded newspaper and held it up. "You really ought to be more cautious . . . I found this upstairs by the door, whither you dropped it." The room was surveyed with quiet satisfaction. "You like my little exhibit?" he asked earnestly. "A fine collection if I do say so myself. There are no others quite like them—literally. Not even was Madame Tussaud, with all her *mementos mori*, so honoured as we.

"Take the one on the end, for instance, the gent nearest you. Dr William Palmer, the 'Prince of Poisoners'. You might recall the name yourself, as he was hanged only eight years ago in '56, for doing away with numerous relatives. He was even guilty of infanticide, all to collect the money from their insurance policies in order to pay his debts. Truly a master of the art, experimenting with everything from strychnine to tartar emetic and prussic acid."

His eyes burned with a strange intensity. The four fiendish figures gloated from their cobwebbed coverts.

"Next is John Bishop of Shoreditch, confessed grave robber and murderer of several women and children. He had a rather unusual method for their demise: he would lower his victims down a deep well at the rear of his house, laboriously, head first until they drowned. He too swung, in 1832.

"Beside him is a fellow by the name of John Williams, young deckhand who, one blustery night in 1812, took a long ripping chisel and butchered an entire household without apparent motive. Directly he also killed and mutilated three members of another family. A crazed, homicidal maniac. In short order he was captured, but ne'er brought to trial because he committed suicide in his cell. He was buried at a crossroads with a stake through his heart, where I promptly 'acquired' the remains, as I did the others.

"Ah, but no such distinguished company of mass-murderers would be complete without my other friend there, the skeleton fondling the garrotte." He chuckled softly. "Perhaps you two have already made acquaintance—'twas he you brought to me in that bag, rescued from the thief Hooks. A bit bewildered? Then allow me to elaborate with a story, as not altogether found in any newspaper."

He folded his arms and casually leaned against the wall, but remaining close to the sole exit.

"Back in 1827, there was a prominent, respected anatomist teaching at Edinburgh University in Scotland. His name was Dr Robert Knox. It was a quiet custom for surgeons to procure cadavers for classroom dissection; whenever available the unclaimed bodies of paupers, waifs, executed felons and the like were used, but frequently these were of insufficient number, and so the professor discreetly offered ten pounds apiece for bodies brought to him. Such typical rewards proved a generous incentive for 'resurrectionists' to pay nocturnal visits on the boneyard, and 'tis known even crooked undertakers would periodically sell bodies from their parlours and later inter a closed coffin weighed with bricks. But the vigilance with which burial grounds throughout the country were watched rendered such ghoulish exploits more hazardous every day. Hence, a black market for fresh specimens.

"Along about this time two men named William Burke and William Hare and their prostitute 'wives' moved into a boardinghouse in West Port belonging to one of the women. One day an elderly highlander died there, still in arrears on his rent. They decided to sell the body to settle the account.

This was so easy the foursome hit on the scheme of luring in only aged, sickly lodgers. However, they grew impatient of the waiting it entailed and began slipping their tenants laudanum to drink, and afterwards smothering them. These criminal pastimes developed into a lucrative livelihood, but eventually even this was not enough, and greed drove them into the nighted streets for more potential victims. Over a two-year period nigh eight and twenty corpses were provided Dr Knox.

"It so happened the professor had an unofficial assistant, before the latter became involved in his own line of work a twelve-month later. 'Twas he who on many occasions inconspicuously accepted and paid the two sack-'em-ups for the goods delivered to him at number ten Surgeons' Square, on behalf of the doctor.

"Throughout the entire episode the medical man and his apprentice were never fully cognizant of the terrible misdeeds actually being committed—that is, not until the end. True, it was Knox's policy to ask no questions, but the subjects were not supposed to have been wantonly murdered and transferred to him ofttimes still warm.

"Finally the whole bloody business was unearthed when a pair of neighbours perchance stumbled upon a recent victim. The two women endeavoured to bribe them, but they went at once to the authorities.

"Effort was made to save the rags of prestige for the medical profession by leaving Dr Knox out of the investigation and scraping together such scraps of evidence as might be obtainable from other sources— primarily the testimony of Hare who, although probably the more ruthless, turned King's evidence and accepted a pardon in reciprocation for his disclosures against his consort, whom he brazenly denounced as the perpetrator.

"In any case, the indirect complicity of the good doctor could not be hushed up completely, being repeatedly assailed in the press, and while formally exonerated of all charges of wrongdoing, the incident led to his professional and social ruin for many years. Even so, not once did he ever divulge his loyal aide's implication in the dangerous affair. This was very fortunate for the younger, because carefully hidden on one of the last bodies imparted to him—not having been stripped of clothing as usual—he discovered a full money belt that had been overlooked, lined with bank notes amounting to a tidy sum. And no one ever knew. Knox died two years ago, but never outlived the taunting nursery rhyme:

> *Burke's the butcher. Hare's the thief.*
> *And Knox the boy who buys the beef.*
> *Hang Burke, banish Hare.*
> *Burn Knox in Surgeons' Square.*

"Only one of the two women was taken into custody, but not convicted. Disguised as a man, she shipped to Australia. As a result of several lynching attempts the other was extradited to somewhere in Ireland. Hare, not so easily dealt with, was smuggled out of gaol as 'Mr Black' and put aboard a south-bound mail coach. He was chased by a mob at Dumfries but cunningly dodged them. Out of vindictiveness he tried to blackmail Dr Knox's attendant with threats to expose him, till presently he disappeared and was not seen or heard from again, except for an unverified story that he was recognized by fellow workers who threw him in a limekiln, condemning him to the harried life of a maimed, sightless beggar peddling matches in the gutters of London.

"As for Burke, he was silenced when he did the gallows dance before a bloodthirsty crowd soon after the trial. His body was publicly dismembered, then pickled in brine and stored for future reference. Later his skeleton was reassembled for display at the University's museum. There Hooks, on my orders, substituted it with another, but upon returning to London he became distrustful and wanted payment made on his own terms. You saw to that little detail.

"Shortly thereafter I heard an obscure rumour that Hare had somehow ended up in Bedlam. Because physicians often dissect the brains of dead lunatics in seeking the cause of insanity or insomuch as their bodies are otherwise molested, I could not take the chance. I had no qualms whatsoe'er about bringing him back myself, but again, why take any unnecessary risks? As events turned out, the rumour was true, and now thanks to you here he is safely home to stay. I have reserved the empty niche over there for him. I was considering extending a noose down around his neck . . . justice done at last. Bizarre but effective. A capital idea, do you not agree?"

I just stood there wondering what the madman would do next, and whether or not to attempt a rush for the steps.

A wry smile again touched the corners of his lips, a purr of mockery in his voice.

"Well, by now you have surely surmised who I am, and why the unnatural and admittedly morbid interest in my two corpse-vending friends. Yes, *I* was Dr Knox's secret assistant! So you see, I have a few skeletons in my own closet . . . albeit these long years in my profession have inured my conscience, if not my—shall we call it obsession?—with an unsavoury past."

I gazed into his bottomless eyes, cold and hard as a gravestone, and knew it was true.

"But alas," he said darkly, "it seems I have yet another bony hidling to hang in my closet. I should have realized your inquisitiveness would be your own undoing, that you would never suit my purposes. I felt a maudlin kind of kinship, because you were intelligent and had pluck—but I suppose I was really wanting a witless errand-boy who might keep his nose where it belongs." He smashed a vial of alcohol against the wall. "Ah well, such errors in judgement can be easily corrected . . ."

Then he came at me with the jagged neck of the bottle.

Wildly I tore the sconce from its brace and threw it at him, searing his arm and knocking him off balance so that he slipped on the wet fragments of glass and fell to the floor. I dashed over his prostrate body and pulled one of the cabinets down on top of him as I did so, leaving him in a daze while frantically bolting up out of the cellar and into the street.

Fifteen minutes later I located a constable.

My erstwhile employer was gone by the time the police arrived at the scene, his establishment deserted save for the unspeakable horrors brooding balefully in the basement. Upon a thorough inspection of the premises they also discovered a somewhat sizeable cache of currency carefully hoarded away amongst some personal effects . . . his inheritance. A systematic search was likewise conducted in the immediate neighbourhood but nothing helpful became of it. No, it appeared he made good his escape, and fled the area altogether.

Be that as it may, Inspector Winters, the chief constable, believed different. Pointing out the large amount of money left behind, he felt the fugitive had either forgotten or momentarily forsaken it in his panic to get away, but was in all likelihood contriving plans to retrieve it as soon as possible since it would be needed to carry him a comfortable distance and in assuming a new identity. Probably, he said, the man temporarily went into hiding somewhere in the general vicinity, simply waiting for all the hubbub to subside. In the meantime they were on the watch for him and would alert surrounding boroughs and districts with a full description. Other than that there was not much else they could do at the present. Of course I had related my whole sordid story from beginning to end over several strong cups of tea, whilst the inspector jotted notes and then thanked me, assuring they would keep me posted if anything of significance was turned up.

Almost a week later, however, Jeremy Sloan was still eluding the police, with not a shred of evidence yet uncovered.

Then something began to writhe in the dark pockets of my mind, and a number of confusing questions came to surface. I was puzzled as to why the Yard had taken no action against Alfred Cobbs, the Bedlam guard. Perhaps it was due to the fact that all efforts were currently focused on the search itself, and moreover, because they already suspected his involvement in prior breakouts from Bedlam; and although infrequent, few were ever apprehended, or so one of the constables informed me. But if that was the case why were formal charges not brought against him long ago? Unless, I presume, they had been unable to actually prove anything.

Still, there was something else, worming its way from out my subconscious—something that had been overlooked on my part, of which the police were not wholly aware.

Finally it struck me. With much difficulty I was eventually able to trace down a cabby who claimed that he did recall having been engaged a week ago by a man of Sloan's description, taking him straight to Howlbury Street—just one block from Bedlam!

I went forthwith to the police and revealed this corroborative item of information. A detail was dispatched immediately to the asylum. When they returned, I was still waiting nervously in Inspector Winters' office.

A stocky, ruddy-faced bobby came in to give his report.

"Yes sir, we found 'im there allright. Blimey, who would've ever thought it? We've also brought back Cobbs. It seems our man Sloan sought refuge there, figuring it would be the safest place to cool 'is 'eels, and promised to pay the guard for concealing 'im. An old storage room behind 'is keeper's quarters was no longer being used, so 'e'd cleverly sealed it off years ago by disguising it. We came across it by accident."

He shot a peculiar look at his superior, and I was left with the funny feeling of missing out on something.

"But what about Cobbs," I enquired, "why was he not arrested earlier? Someone said—"

The younger man started to evade my question, until the Inspector broke in.

"Go ahead and tell him. I don't really think he'll fancy to go about sharing this with anyone."

The other hesitated, took a deep breath, and continued.

"Yes, it's true what one of the other officers told you—that we've tried to keep our eye on 'im for a long time . . . something directly connected with the apparent escapes. So it's rather an ironic twist of fate your employer should fall in with this Cobbs fellow; because, neither could we establish sufficient proof. Now, though . . ."

He left the sentence hanging, and a slight grimace on his face goaded me to ask one more question.

"Of just what crime was he suspicioned?"

In answer he produced a canvas bag from behind his back and emptied the grisly but recognizable contents on the table before me, his single word sickening my soul.

". . . Cannibalism."

Evelyn K. Martin

NIRVANA

Nirvana . . .
Where I walk alone
And drink great breaths
From mouths of trees,
And listen to droning
Honeybees
Like tigers on the wing.

Nirvana . . .
Where the horse-cropped grass
Is prickly to my feet.
Great owl-eyes
Peer from the scarecrow trees.
I listen to the rustling
Ghostly breeze
A spectre in the night.

There is a facade
The world can see
Another me,
Lost in the crowd.
But inside, deep,
Where none can see
A soundless cry of agony . . .
I cannot weep aloud.

Garry Kilworth

ISLAND WITH THE STINK OF GHOSTS

Garry Kilworth first appeared in Fantasy Tales *last year with a story about an insane toilet. The tale which follows is completely different. It shows the versatility of this master of the short genre story, his preferred medium. His work has been widely published, most recently collected in* Dark Hills, Hollow Clocks *(faery fantasy for young readers, from Methuen) and* The Songbirds of Pain *(Gollancz/Unwin). Garry is the author of more than a dozen novels, several of them for younger readers. Some of his recent books are* Midnight's Sun, The Third Dragon *and* The Drowners, *while next year Grafton will publish his mainstream end-of-empire novel, set in the last years of colonial rule in Aden,* The Gulli-Gulli Man, *and a SF and fantasy collection,* In the Country of Tattooed Men. *Recent stories have been reprinted in* Best New Horror 2, The Year's Best Fantasy and Horror: Fourth Annual Collection *and* The Best of the Rest 1990, *and he is currently at work on a Celtic fantasy entitled* Frost Dancers.

The Chinese jetty clans, who ruled the waterfronts along Penang's Georgetown harbour, fostered the myth that their hawkers had been responsible for its formation. It was said that chicken fat, glutinous rice, fishheads, *hokkien* noodles, prawn shells, and other waste matter, had gathered together in a stretch of still water between the currents and had formed the foundations of the floating island. Sargasso had rooted itself in the rich oils and savoury spices, on top of which gathered soil from the mainland. A rainforest had grown from its earth.

The island was about three miles off the Malaysian coast and was held precariously in place by the fronds of seaweed rooted in the ocean floor. No one, not even the ancient Wan Hooi, who ran a clan *curry mee* stall on the Larong Salamat, could remember the time when the island had not been there. Wan Hooi was the oldest hawker on Penang, but it was pointed out that he had only been around for a hundred years. The clans had been using the harbour as a waste bin for more than a thousand.

Whenever there was an onshore breeze, a sickly, perfumed odour wafted over from the island. This smell, according to both Malays and Chinese, was the stink of ghosts rotting—or to be more accurate, the odour of decaying souls. The body, when it decomposes, has a foul smell. Therefore, it seemed logical that a putrefying soul should have a sweet, cloying scent. The island was the burial ground for malefactors and murderers, whose punishment after death was for the corrupt soul to remain with the body, and rot within it.

These beliefs had little to do with religion, but came from a deeply-rooted local superstition, such as is found in any region: a myth from earlier, darker minds, when reason and evidence were less important than fear.

Fishermen gave the island a wide berth, and only the old gravedigger, Lo Lim Hok, set foot upon the place.

Ralph Leeman, an Englishman in his late twenties, was one of those who witnessed the event on a hot, sultry June evening, when the island broke loose from its natural mooring. Not that

168

How stupid he had been! He had allowed the island to feed his guilt.
(Art: Martin McKenna)

169

there was any drama, for there was no sound and little fuss. The island simply detached itself from its anchoring reeds and began drifting down the Malacca Straits, which runs between Indonesia and Malaysia. Possibly heavy rains in Thailand, to the north, had been responsible for a strong swell. This had resulted in a momentary change in the direction of the main current, the East Monsoon Drift, which put pressure on the island. That was Leeman's theory.

Leeman was on secondment to the Malaysian Harbour Authority from the British Coastal Service. Alone in the observation tower, he had been studying the erratic behavior of a large motor launch, when he was suddenly aware that the island was moving. He watched it for a few moments, as it passed a distant marker buoy.

"Good God! Stinker's on the move."

He immediately made a call to his superior.

Sumi Pulau, the harbourmaster, arrived at the tower thirty minutes later, having fought his way through the Georgetown traffic. He studied the island through binoculars and expressed his amazement and concern. His English, like that of many educated Malays, was extremely good.

"Directly in the shipping lane. We'll have to do something about it immediately. It'll be dark soon. Got any suggestions?"

Leeman had already been considering the problem and gave his opinion.

"We could attach tugboats to it and tow it to the mainland— but given the nature of the island—the fact that it's a graveyard, I'm not sure the coastal villages would want it on their doorstep."

Pulau nodded.

"Yes, and in any case, *I'm* not sure tugs would do it. Might take something bigger. That's a pretty sizeable piece of land out there."

"My second thought was that we could blow it out of the water with high explosives—but I'm worried about the jetties and the stilt-houses. An explosion might create a floodwave."

"Not to mention the fact that we would have corpses washing up on the tourist beaches . . ."

"So," continued Leeman, eager to impress, "I suggest we just let it float down the straits. We put a boat in front and behind, to warn other craft of the shipping hazard. I've been judging its speed, using the marker buoys and by my reckoning the island should reach Singapore in thirteen days. Then it can be towed into open water and disposed of . . ."

The harbourmaster looked thoughtful.

". . . and I have a final suggestion," said Leeman.

"Which is?"

"That we put a caretaker on the island, to place and maintain lights, fore and aft. This man could keep in radio contact with the accompanying boats and inform them of any problems. The sort of thing I envisage is the island running aground on a sandbank—which might solve all our worries—or breaking up in a storm. That sort of thing."

Pulau scratched his head thoughtfully.

"I like it all except the caretaker. I'm not sure it's necessary to have someone actually *on* the island. It would have to be you, you know. I wouldn't get any of my men near the place. *The island with the stink of ghosts*—they would die of fright."

"I realize that. Of course, I would volunteer. It would be an additional safety factor."

The harbourmaster smiled at Leeman.

"You're not afraid of ghosts, I take it?"

"Not in the least." Which was not entirely true. The thought of spending thirteen nights in a graveyard was mildly discomforting, but only that. The physical dangers? Well, that part of it might be rewarding.

"Right," said Pulau, suddenly becoming decisive, "that's how we'll play it. I'll call the Minister. You get back to your lodgings and pack what you think you'll need and I'll arrange it. Tent and provisions?"

"And gaslights."

"Of course . . . You really aren't concerned about the

171

supernatural side of it?"

"No."

Leeman looked at the dark mass, moving slowly through the water in the distance. Despite his disbelief, it looked eerie and forbidding. A fishing canoe, one of those traditional craft with modern outboard engines thrusting it obscenely across the water, cut away sharply from the island's path.

"What did they do—most of them? Those murderers buried on the island? It seems a harsh judgement on the dead," he murmured.

"Drug runners," replied Pulau. "You know how we feel about them, here in Malaysia."

A shadow crossed Leeman's mind, painfully. He remembered that drug trafficking carried a mandatory death sentence in Malaysia, for those convicted of the crime. It was, perhaps, one of the reasons why he had chosen to do his secondment in this part of the world.

"I see," he said, quietly.

Pulau regarded him with a quizzical expression.

"Does it make any difference? To you, I mean."

Leeman thought about his younger brother, Pete. Of course it made a difference. The cycle of thoughts which he continually had to fight, to break out of, began whirling in his head. *Not again*, he thought. *Please. Why are there so many reminders? Why can't I be left alone?*

It made a hell of a difference.

"No," he said. "I just wondered, that was all."

On the way to the boarding house, in Lebuh Campbell, he told himself how much he liked it on Penang, in the Far East. He enjoyed the expatriate life, with its accompanying indulgence in a completely different culture. He was an advocate of an older way of life, with values he felt the modern world had wrongly placed aside. In the Far East, you could get closer to such values. They gave one a sense of historical continuity: a connection with the past. He could enjoy it more, if only . . . if only he could throw off the mistakes of the *immediate* past. But they clung to his mind like leeches, sucking it dry . . . He had said *sorry* many, many times, but there were no ears to hear, no one to listen . . . He had run to the Far East in order to get away from the leeches, but that had not been far enough. Here he was, running again, to a small, floating island that had detached itself from the world.

At first he was too busy to allow the sweet fragrance of the island to disturb him. He had to place the calor gas lamps, at either end of the rainforest, involving a mile walk along the shore. Then there was the business of setting up camp (something Pete would have enjoyed): erecting the tent, unpacking provisions, starting a fire and, finally, using the radio transceiver. He reported to the accompanying craft that all was well and he was preparing to bed down for the night.

Once these duties had been accomplished, he had more time to consider his environment.

There were the usual jungle noises, that he had often heard on Penang. There were cicadas which gave out sounds like factory whistles; frogs that bellowed like megaphones; and birds that ran up and down scales as if they were taking some form of musical training.

There were also other sounds: the breeze in the palms and the rippling of water through the thick weed on which the island was based.

Then there was that *smell*.

It was by no means a disagreeable perfume and reminded him of incense, but it seemed so dense as to stain the air with its presence. Perhaps the cause lay in some unusual plant? Then again, it might have come from the thick sargasso which supported the soil and rainforest? That explanation seemed much more likely.

He took a torch and went to the edge of the island, to peer down into the shallows. There was no beach. Instead, a soil bank dropped sharply into the sea, beneath the surface of which he could see the myriad vines of sargassum, knotted

173

together to form a mass of spongy weed. It was alive with sea creatures, mostly eels.

Leeman backed away, a little disconcerted. He was revolted, not by the creatures themselves, but by their numbers. It almost seemed as if the island were a live thing, crawling with tentacles. This, coupled with the thought that there was a great depth of ocean beneath him—a strange sensation until he managed to convince himself that the island was only a raft: a craft fashioned by nature instead of man—made him tread lightly for a while. Once he had got used to the idea that it was in effect nothing more than a platform of weed, a natural Kon Tiki, carried along by the current, he managed to keep his imagination under control.

He slept very little that first night, the smell overpowering his desire for rest. He rose, once or twice, to watch the lights drift by on the mainland, and gained some comfort from those of the accompanying craft.

When morning came, sweltering but happily blessed with bright sunlight, he was able to explore his surroundings without the intrusion of irrational fears, of rotting souls. The rainforest, half-a-mile wide, was much like any other he had seen on Penang. It was dense, its undergrowth and canopy formed of a thousand different plants of which he knew few by name. He recognised the frangipani trees of course, regarded by the Chinese as unlucky, and tamarind, and various types of palm. He knew there would be snakes amongst the vines, and large spiders quivering on the underside of waxy leaves, but these did not bother him overmuch. He had sprayed the area around the tent with paraffin, which would keep any wildlife away. Pete would have been terrified of them, of course, but then Pete was not with him.

He managed to busy himself with small tasks that occupied his mind to a degree, but there was no ignoring the smell. He recalled Pulau's statement, about the graves containing the bodies of drug runners, and felt sick at heart as the guilt washed through him. He kept telling himself that he was in

174

no way to blame. He had not known what the launches were carrying: *still* did not know. He guessed their cargo consisted of contraband of some kind, but surely not narcotics? It could have been anything. Booze? Cigarettes? But did he honestly believe that people smuggled such things into Britain any more? The real money was in heroin and cocaine. Organised crime syndicates did not bother with tobacco and alcohol. And they had been organised. Oh, yes. His payments had arrived, on the dot, every month. A plain brown envelope full of crisp banknotes. *Very* efficient, he thought bitterly. And all he had to do was turn a blind eye.

He began weeping, softly, as he stoked his fire.

"The bastards," he said. "The bloody, fucking bastards. They killed my baby brother . . ."

The island's peculiar cloying scent became an irritant over the next day or two. It was like a spirit in constant attendance and it bothered him a lot. He thought about the graves and wondered about their number. Were they unmarked, or were there headstones? Perhaps his tent was sited directly over a murderer's corpse, its putrefied flesh and corroding soul exuding opposing, distinctive odours? He dismissed the idea. The layer of soil was too thin near the shore. He could see the white stains of the saltwater, seeping through the grass.

He studied these white patches, with loathing. They were threatening, simply because they were reminders of white powder. They demanded his attention, and once they had it, initiated that terrible cycle of thoughts which had his mind reeling. How swiftly nature turned from friend, to enemy . . .

"How long have I been here?" he asked the boat.

"Five days," came the reply.

Another eight to go. The mosquitoes were biting well. (He preferred to think of them as biting, rather than sticking their needle mouths into his skin. That was too much like being injected, with a hypodermic . . .) It meant he had to spend time

175

with his body, inspecting it, ministering to its minor problems.

He began doing all tasks with elaborate precision: making rituals of them, taking pains to perfect methods. Pete used to like rituals. When they were children, sharing a bedroom, he used to make fun of Pete, who would fold his clothes in just the same way, every night. It was supposed to keep away the bogey men. Pete had liked high church too, because of its mystical rituals. Then later—not so much later—those other rituals: the strings of powder—chasing the dragon. He should have seen all this in Pete, earlier. Done something to . . . to divert the course.

Sometimes he found himself staring at the forest, that hid the graves, that breathed the scent of the dead. He discovered something which he decided no other living person had yet noticed: that shadows were not all of the same thickness. There were those that lay black and heavy, rarely moving. There were those, slightly thinner, that changed position and shape lethargically. Then there were the younger shadows, like smoky movements on the grass.

He found he had power over the shadows. Those he did not like, he removed with his machete. He gave birth to new shadows, using mats of woven palm leaves. Screens and shields were placed around the camp area, so that they cast their dark shades on the ugly white stains, neutralizing them. The artist in him helped to create a territory in which the reminders were few.

Then it rained, battering down his palm thatch shields. The new, unprotected shadows, drained away in rivulets.

He passed his reports at the specified times, but avoided social discourse. The reason, if he asked himself at all, was that disembodied voices from the outside world tended to emphasise his solitude, rather than provide relief from it.

He found the heat of the day extremely oppressive, and often fell asleep in his tent of an afternoon, to wake in a pool of sweat as the evening approached. Though he had plenty of drinking water, he lost so much body fluid in the airless atmosphere of the tent, he began to develop dehydration headaches.

"Nine days."

It rained heavily for the third time since he had arrived on the island. The fire was difficult to light. He used many matches, and when he looked down at their spent forms, he saw with surprise that they made a word. He did not like the word, was angry with it, and kicked it out of understanding. After his rebellion, night and day took it on themselves to confuse him. They lost their sense of rhythm, their timing. He would lift the tent flap to find darkness where he expected light. Or the other way around. Such happenings only served to further erode his trust in the world. There were other problems. He had ceased to breathe air. There was none on the island. He breathed only the perfume that had replaced it. The fragrance was corrosive, staining him internally. He tried making masks to filter out its impurities, but there was no mesh fine enough to prevent the sickly odour from entering his lungs.

"Ten days."

How stupid he had been! He had allowed the island to feed his guilt, keep the cycle of thoughts turning until he was physically sick, until he was so locked into himself that only a major event, like a rainstorm, could break him out. He now dismissed such ideas as weak and foolish. It was up to him to resist, not succumb, to the island's pressures. He was the master of the island. He told it this fact, in no uncertain terms.

On the twelfth night, they called him, waking him from a muzzy sleep to say that the lights at the rear of the island had failed. He took a torch and trudged along the coastline, to relight the gas. On the return journey, he stumbled off the path, into the jungle, and found himself on a well-worn track. He followed it to a central clearing, where gravestones sprouted from the

177

tall grass. The scent was overpowering here, in the glade. He turned, to leave the place quickly.

At the edge of the clearing he stumbled over an ovoid object. He shone his torch on it. It was a durian. Since arriving on the island, he had deliberately avoided eating any of its produce, though rambutan grew in abundance. The durian at his feet had split on impact with the ground and lay open. Leeman had developed a taste, almost a craving, for this addictive fruit, which the locals regarded as a delicacy. It had a sweet flavour, but highly offensive smell. Someone had once described it as like eating honey in a public toilet.

In his half-asleep state he picked up a piece of the durian and sniffed the white flesh. For a moment the perfume of the island was swamped by the foul stink of the durian. Without thinking, he took a bite and swallowed. It tasted good.

He realized, almost instantly, what he had done. The green dragon had seduced him. He stared around him, in horror, at the graves which the roots of the durian tree must surely have penetrated, feeding there. The pressure built in his head, until he felt his skull was splitting. A numbness overcame his legs and he lost his balance, falling to the ground, where he lay trembling violently. He heard himself shouting, "Oh, God . . ." over and over again. He had tried to ride the back of the green dragon, and had lost control. It had carried him to savage days and cruel nights, working insidiously from within him.

He crawled back to camp on his hands and knees and once there, fell into a deep sleep. His dreams were sour.

They came for him the following morning: Singapore was in sight. He felt drugged and heavy headed, as though he had spent some time in a smoke-filled room. Sympathetic hands helped him to the boat.

"What about the island?" he asked, as they sailed away.

"There's a dredger ready, to tow it out into open waters," a sailor replied.

Then someone asked him, "Are you all right? You look ill—are you sick?"

178

He did not feel sick, and shook his head.

"I found it hard to sleep." They would understand that. "I'm okay now—now that it's over. That place could send you mad—was it only thirteen days? It seemed much longer."

"You don't look crazy," the sailor smiled, "just exhausted." He tried to smile back.

"Yes—tired, that's all. I seem to have done nothing but slept, but I'm still tired. It gets to be a habit, when you're on your own."

"I'm glad it wasn't me. I hate being lonely."

On the journey across the water, he cleared his lungs, breathing deeply. Familiar odours were beginning to reach him, from the harbour. The smell of garbage around the sampans; of cooking from the hawker stalls; of decaying fruit. To Leeman, they were clean smells.

The cycle of thoughts, the arguments that had raged continuously in his brain, had ceased. He had reached a dreadful conclusion. He was no better than those men in the island's graves. In fact he was worse. He had been responsible, even if indirectly, for the death of his own brother. While he had been collecting payments for allowing certain launches to go unreported, past his observation tower on an English rivermouth, Pete had been dying of an overdose of heroin. He had not even known his brother was an addict: that was how much he had cared.

Not wanting to return on the boat, he booked into a hotel in Singapore town, close to the harbour. Once in his room, he undressed and threw the shirt and shorts into the waste bin. Then he showered himself, carefully, soaping his skin for three hours. As he shaved, his breath misted the mirror, so that his eyes were hidden from him.

Later, he went down to the bar and drank down two straight whiskies that hardly touched his throat. Although he would have preferred to keep his own company, an American began to talk to him, and he found himself responding. After several more drinks, he told the man about the ghosts of the island and the sweet stink of their souls.

"Embalming fluid," said the American. "Take it from me—I've smelt the stuff. It carries. Boy does it carry. My brother-in-law was an undertaker . . ."

"I expect you're right," said Leeman.

When he was sufficiently drunk, he went out and began to walk the streets. He needed a little more comfort than the American could offer. He wanted arms around him and a soft voice, talking nonsense. There is nothing more comforting than empty talk, when you want to keep your head clear.

He found a young woman, outside a bar, and bought her a few drinks before she took him home to bed. She chattered the whole while, even as she stripped, about her relations, about the difficulties of making ends meet, about the meanness of her landlord. He let her words wash over him, without interrupting.

Then, while they were making love, she told him that he was good. He was very, very good. He looked good, he tasted good, he *smelled* good . . .

Leeman threw her out of the bed, savagely, and screamed abuse at her. The frightened girl grabbed her sarong and ran out into the night. He dressed quickly, and left.

He walked the streets. He thought about the island's air and the fruits of its earth. It was in him, in his system. He could not scour it from him with words. It had breathed its breath into his murderer's lungs. It had tricked him into ingesting its offspring.

He found another bar and while he was being served a drink, asked the young Chinese waiter to smell his skin. The boy hurried away, without a backward glance. Leeman stared after him bleakly, then studied the sweat on his forearm, coming through his pores.

He brought the back of his hand up to his face . . . slowly . . . convinced that time was his terrible enemy, that time was in league with corruption, leaving nothing in its wake but the faint odour of hell's flowers.

Samantha Lee

JELLY ROLL BLUES

Samantha Lee's most recent appearance in Fantasy Tales *was
'Scoop' last year. Her short stories have been published widely,
including five tales broadcast on London's Capital Radio. She
has written a fantasy trilogy, which appeared in the early 1980s,
and more recently* Childe Rolande *was her seventh published
novel. Fantasy and horror forthcoming include a story in Charles
L. Grant's* Final Shadows *anthology and a long poem in* Now We
Are Sick *edited by Neil Gaiman and Stephen Jones. Between
acting jobs, Samantha has been exploring mainstream fiction,
with several acceptances in women's magazines. The story you
are about to read rounds out this number of* Fantasy Tales *on a
somewhat lighter note than usual . . .*

T he Barmaid, a pulchritudinous piece in her late twenties,
polishing glasses with all the application of the terminally bored,
looked up in surprise as Pete came in, shaking the snow off his
trenchcoat.

"What a night," he said, ankling through the deep pile carpet
to perch himself on a stool. "Give us a double brandy, love, and
have one yourself, will you?"

The Barmaid, whose name was Raquel, favoured Pete with

a toothsome smile.

"Don't mind if I do, Sir," she said. "I'll have a G and T if it's all the same to you."

"Make it a large one," said Pete, generously. "After all, it *is* Christmas Eve."

Raquel turned her attention to the relevant optics and Pete noted with appreciation the pleasing spectacle of the barmaid's voluptuous bottom struggling to escape from its skin-tight satin sheath.

"Quiet tonight," he observed, shifting in his seat to get a better view of the premises.

Quiet was an understatement.

Pete was the only person in the place.

And he was damned if he could figure out why. For the Holly Bush, judged on the drinking man's pub scale of one to ten, was undoubtedly a good nine and three quarters.

The lighting was muted, the music mellow. The plush chairs, well-padded (like Raquel) and astrew with plump cushions, almost begged to be sat in. The panelled walls, hung with horse-brasses and hunting-prints, smelled faintly of polish, as did the dark oak tables each complete with a gleaming ashtray. In one corner, an enormous log fire crackled cheerily, the light from it's flame reflecting, like coloured fireflies, in the baubles on the adjacent Christmas Tree. In short, the Holly Bush was precisely what every Tavern should be. Cosy, warm, welcoming. A place where a man could relax at the end of a hard day. The total antithesis, in fact, of those juke-boxed, neon-lit, pin-ball parlours, awash with warm beer and unpleasant company, which so often passed as public houses in the so-called enlightened eighties.

"Always quiet," Raquel confided, mournfully.

She plonked the serving of dark gold brandy in front of her solitary customer and leant her elbows on the counter, affording Pete a grandstand view of her spectacular breasts. Firelight flickered in the dark pupils of her whiskey coloured eyes and Pete reflected that, as the Holly Bush was to pubs, so Raquel was to Barmaids—well-nigh perfect.

"Can't understand it," he said, lifting his glass and allowing the smooth spirit to slick down his throat like warm honey. "Nice pub. Nice company." He winked and Raquel had the grace to blush, taking a hasty sip of gin and tonic to cover her confusion. "Nice brandy." Pete had another swallow to prove his point. "What's the problem? Place ought to be bursting at the seams."

"Don't I know it," pouted Raquel. "Used to be too. Then the Rose and Garter down the road pinched our piano player. Offered him more money if you please and he just upped and left, taking all the customers with him."

She tossed her raven locks in scorn at such disloyalty and Pete tut-tutted his disapproval, remembering the saloon he had passed at the far end of the street. It had, indeed, been bulging with seasonal revellers and a maudlin voice, crucifying *My Way*, had filtered out through the dirty windows to the accompaniment of a tinny piano.

"Now I won't get my Christmas bonus," said Raquel, plaintively, and a tear welled in her big brown eyes and fell, with a plop, onto her cleavage.

Pete wiped it away with his handkerchief.

Raquel's breath, warm and sweet with the scent of juniper berries, fanned his cheek with the promise of infinite possibilities.

"We'd better do something about that," announced Pete.

So saying, he groped in the cavernous pocket of his trenchcoat and produced, rather as a magician might spirit a rabbit from a hat, a tiny little man.

Raquel's luscious mouth dropped open and her wide eyes stretched even wider. As a Barmaid of some experience, she'd seen many a strange sight in her day, but never anything to compare with this small but perfect mannikin, immaculately clad in white tie and tails and smoking a strong cheroot. He stood just slightly over one foot tall.

"Hi georgeous," said the apparition. "You gotta piano in this joint?"

"In the corner," croaked Raquel and proceeded to award herself a double gin, double quick.

Pete meanwhile, delighted with the effect he was having, crossed to the baby grand, raised the lid and deposited his minuscule companion on the keys.

As soon as his toes touched middle C, the little chap began to play, tripping the light fantastic in a manner not unreminiscent of a midget Fred Astaire. He twirled and pranced, sashayed and do-se-doed, bucking and winging up and down the instrument like a tiny, tapping, terpsichoreal tornado.

And the sound he produced was sheer magic.

The mellifluous mood-music circled the salon, caressing the ear like liquid silk, then it meandered out into the snow-clad street, a siren-call beckoning the weary traveller home.

Before he had finished the second chorus of *Putting on the Ritz*, the first customers had begun to trickle in.

An hour later, the pub was jammed.

By the end of the evening, Raquel had had to S.O.S. several times for extra bar staff and her Christmas bonus was assured—in triplicate.

Later . . . much later . . . having disposed of the more immediate urgencies, Raquel turned over on her side and posed Pete the question she'd been dying to ask all evening.

"Where on earth did you find him?"

Pete glanced contentedly towards the dressing-table drawer, where the little piano man snored soundly amongst Raquel's unmentionables.

"Funny story, that," he said. "Happened on Christmas Eve, strangely enough. Couple of years ago, now. Oxford Street, it was. Usual crush of last minute shoppers. Bedlam, to tell you the truth. Traffic was murder. Anyway, there I was, just about to cross the road, when I spot this old bloke, falling apart at the seams he was, dithering about on the kerb, scared to go over. So I gave him a hand, didn't I?

"And guess what . . . when we got to the other side, he

looked at me—sly like—and he says . . .

"'Young man, that's the first act of human kindness that's been shown to me in many a long year. I'm not really an old tramp,' he says, 'as you might have deduced from my appearance. Actually,' he says, 'I'm Father Christmas and, as a reward, you can have one wish. Name it. Anything your heart desires . . .'

"And perhaps it was because the traffic was so loud . . . or maybe the old bloke was a bit hard of hearing . . . whatever . . . I ended up with a thirteen inch pianist!"

ACKNOWLEDGEMENTS